MIAMI HOMICIDE

BY

John C. Dalglish

2016

VALENTINE'S DAY

Saturday, February 14

Collins Avenue
Miami Beach
10:45 p.m.

Running from its beginning in Key West, and going by various names as it wound its way up the Atlantic Coast of Florida, Highway A1A eventually ended on Amelia Island, just south of the Georgia border. For most of that distance, it was referred to as the strip, but longtime residents of Miami called it Collins Avenue.

Teenagers Tricia and Bobby were enjoying their favorite date-night routine, made extra special by the fact it was Valentine's Day. The warm evening was also a treat, as night temperatures could drop into the fifties that time of year, but that night was still in the seventies.

Bobby turned his black Ford Mustang off Collins Avenue and into one of the public parking lots along the beach. They got out and retrieved a blanket from the trunk, locked the car, then walked hand-in-hand toward the ocean. Tricia walked close to him, one arm looped through his while the other held his hand. He loved when she clung to him in such an affectionate way.

A small path of white sand led between tall brush on either side, opening up to a wide moonlit expanse, which in turn gave way to the surf pounding against it. The waves were a non-stop sound of restlessness, matched by the fire in their own hearts, pushing Bobby to break into a run toward the water.

Tricia raced to catch up, finally running into him as he stopped by the water's edge. She wrapped her arms around his neck and they kissed, alone on the beach. They'd stopped too close to the water, and a wave soaked their shoes, the chill putting an end to the embrace.

Bobby looked toward the south and pointed. "There it is. Let's go."

Slowly now, they walked together to the large lifeguard station. Two stories off the beach, it was a glass observation tower surrounded by a wooden deck. The area below was a covered sanctuary, usually filled with rescue boards and buoys, but empty at night.

As Bobby spread the blanket out, the light from the moon was blocked, and they found themselves in the familiar darkness of their favorite spot. Bobby lay down and reached his hand toward her. “Join me?”

Tricia was about to oblige when a sound, like a vehicle door closing, stopped her. At that moment, something caught her eye. Not twenty feet from where they were, she saw the form of a person. “Bobby! I think someone’s over there.”

He lay on his back, smiling up at her. “No way! We’re alone.”

She wasn’t appeased. “I’m not kidding, Bobby. Look.”

Bobby rolled over on his side and peered in the direction she indicated. “Tricia, there’s nobody...” Then he saw the form too, and got to his feet. “Stay here.”

He moved slowly toward the dark shape while pulling out his cell phone to use as a light. It wasn’t his desire to rain on another guy’s parade, and if there were two people instead of one, he’d feel foolish. “Hello?”

Waiting a few seconds longer, and seeing no movement at all, he pushed forward to where he could get a good look.

It’s just a sleeping woman.

He was about to turn around and make his way back to Tricia as quietly as possible when he accidentally pushed a button on his phone. The screen lit up, illuminating the woman's naked body, and the look of death frozen in her eyes.

Bobby staggered backward, tripped into the sand, then clawed his way back up. Running to Tricia, he grabbed her hand and dragged the startled girl after him. "Come on!"

"What is it?"

"A body!"

Home of
Detective Eva Hernandez
Little Havana
11:15 p.m.

It had become a habit of hers to try and pick up the phone before the second ring. She failed this morning. Glancing at the clock as she put it to her ear, Detective Eva Hernandez already knew it was bad news. The digital 11:15 barely registered through the fog of sleep.

Most parents dread the call in the middle of the night because it probably meant bad news about their kids, but Eva had a different perspective. To her, a late night call meant somebody had left this Earth under suspicious circumstances, and they needed help figuring out how and why.

“Hello?”

“Eva?”

“I’m afraid so. What have you got, Luis?”

“Dead body, Haulover Park.”

“More specific?”

“On the beach, second guard station south of the lighthouse tower.”

“Okay. See you in twenty.”

She hung up and dragged herself out of bed. Going out into the hall, she went to her mother’s door and opened it slowly. “Mama?”

There was a stirring of sheets on the bed. “Si?”

“I have a call.”

“Si.”

Eva closed the door and returned to her room. Ten minutes later, she was in her car headed for Haulover Park.

Haulover Beach Park
Miami
11:45 p.m.

Detective Luis Moreno has long since stopped being amazed by his partner. It didn't matter if it was noon or midnight, she always managed to arrive looking prepared and put together.

Nearly as tall as him, her jet-black hair was usually parted on one side and swept into a long ponytail that would occasionally fall forward over one shoulder. Her dark eyes and mocha skin were always highlighted by a small set of stud earrings and light pink lip gloss.

Despite her looks, there was never any doubt as to the real reason behind her success. She was the consummate professional; from the word "go" on any case, she was all business with both suspects and victims. She could alternate between warmth and intensity at will, depending on who she was dealing with at the moment. Luis had felt fortunate to be partnered with her, even if he was a little intimidated at first.

Blue lights flashed in random patterns off the various buildings, clumps of brush, and palm trees, illuminating Detective Hernandez as she approached the scene. Luis met her just behind the guard tower. "Hey, Eva."

"Hey, Luis. What have we got?"

He turned and walked with her toward the body, now lit up by portable halogen spotlights. "Female, late teens to early twenties. Not certain what cause of death was yet, but she's pretty badly beaten up."

"Any weapon?"

He shook his head. "Not that we've found so far. She appeared to be dumped; we found drag marks in the sand from the parking lot to where the body is."

They came up next to the body and Eva got her first look. "Dang, she's a mess. She's naked, can I assume we found no ID?"

"Correct. I've had the perimeter taped off and a search is being done surrounding the entire area."

"Good. Who found her?"

Luis pointed toward the front of the guard station. "A pair of young lovers. They're sitting on the guard station steps."

"Okay. Let's go talk to them."

When the two detectives came around in front of the young couple, the girl jumped noticeably. Eva reached out to steady her. "I'm sorry. I didn't mean to scare you."

The girl managed a weak smile. "It's okay."

"What's your name?"

"Patricia Givens. People call me Tricia."

"How old are you, Tricia?"

"Seventeen."

The detective looked at the young man. "What's your name?"

"Bobby Tucker."

"And how old are you, Bobby?"

"Sixteen."

Luis was taking notes as his partner gently coaxed what she could out of her young witnesses. He wasn't sure how much help they would be, but he doubted they would ever forget *this* walk on the beach.

Eva stepped back and regarded the pair. "You two come down here often?"

They exchanged glances, then nodded.

"How did you come upon the body?"

Bobby gestured at the blanket below the guard station. "We had just arrived here when... Tricia spotted her. I went over to check it out and my cell phone lit up. That's when I realized she was dead."

"Did you see anyone else coming or going from the area before that?"

Bobby shook his head. “We thought we were alone.”

Hernandez turned to Luis. “Have their parents been called?”

“Yeah. They’re on the way.”

“Okay.” She knelt in front of the two teens. “Your parents will have our phone number. If you two think of anything, have them call us, okay?”

They answered in unison. “We will.”

Eva headed back over to where the body lay. Luis instructed a uniformed officer to watch over the teens until their parents arrived, then followed after his partner.

Back at the scene, the familiar form of Dr. Ernesto Fuentes was leaning over the body. A large, round man, he’d been Miami-Dade coroner for over twenty years. With the force nearly four times as long as Luis, he was the only coroner Eva had worked with in her ten-plus years, as well.

Making a personal appearance at a crime scene was one of his trademarks, and despite having plenty of assistants he could send for the body, he preferred to see things firsthand whenever he could. Perpetually unshaven but without a full beard, he wore black-plastic rimmed glasses and surgical scrubs.

Luis wasn’t sure the man owned any clothes of his own. “Hey, Doc.”

"Hey, Luis. Lovely evening."

"Not for our victim."

Fuentes, through much effort, forced himself into a standing position. "Never is for our type of client, is it?"

"Nope."

Eva had her notebook out. "Any sign of sexual assault?"

"Hard to tell yet. I'd prefer to wait until the autopsy, but she's definitely been a victim of physical assault before this. There's a lot of old bruising on her back and buttocks."

A uniformed officer came up behind Luis. "Haven't found anything of interest in the search. There was one couple walking about a hundred yards from here, but they said they arrived just a few minutes ago."

Luis nodded. "Thanks. Well, I guess it's back to the precinct?"

Eva nodded. "We have a general description. We'd better go run it against missing persons reports."

"Okay. I'll meet you there."

Sunday, February 15

Apartment of
Rosie & Gabriela Torres
Fort Myers
7:00 a.m.

"Mom?"

"In here."

Gabriela followed the voice to the back bedroom. She probably didn't need to call out since her mother spent most of her time in bed. Gabriela turned on the light as she entered, drawing a moan from Rosie. "Do you have to do that, Gabby?"

"You can't stay in here all day. Have you eaten?"

"I had a couple of those frozen enchiladas last night."

"I'm gonna make some breakfast for us."

"Oh Gabriela, don't go to any trouble. I'm not very hungry."

"Nonsense. You need to eat to keep your strength up. I'm gonna change while you get up."

Gabby went into the other bedroom, taking her work clothes off and putting on jeans and a t-shirt. In the bathroom, she washed her face and took her long, dark-brown hair out of its workday bun. Just eighteen, Gabby was aware the guys at work found her attractive, much like the boys in high school before she dropped out. She'd been blessed with her mother's wide-set, deep brown eyes and distinct arched eyebrows. Though she'd never met her grandmother, she apparently had her full, wide lips and smile.

Going back to the kitchen, she began putting away the few groceries she'd bought on the way home after her midnight shift. Eventually, Rosie made it out of the bedroom and eased herself onto the couch. Gabby still winced when she watched her mother move around.

"You want anything to drink?"

"Did you make coffee?"

"Yes. It'll be ready in a few minutes."

Gabby's mother had worked as a waitress in the nearby Denny's Restaurant, often pulling double shifts to provide for herself and her daughter, until the night she slipped on a wet floor. Her back had been severely injured, and even though there was a small insurance settlement, Gabby had been the main provider for the two of them ever since.

She fetched the TV remote for Rosie. “Here. Your favorite show should be on soon.”

Rosie was addicted to the Spanish Telenovelas and they seemed to be the only thing she showed interest in anymore. That and her drugs.

She’d been given hydrocodone for the pain of her back injury. When the renewals on the prescription ran out, Rosie had turned to heroin, spending most of her insurance settlement. Gabby hadn’t known until she came home from work one morning to find her mother unconscious on the floor. A call to 9-1-1 had barely saved Rosie’s life.

Rosie had completed a forced rehab program, and since her mother got out, Gabby had been making sure the monthly disability checks didn’t disappear.

She brought her mother a cup of coffee, setting it on the side table. “How’s the pain?”

“Same.”

“Any visitors last night?”

Rosie shook her head slightly and turned her attention to the TV. Asking about “visitors” was Gabby’s way of checking up on her mother. The only guests Rosie would get before going through rehab were the people who sold her heroin.

Gabby left her alone to watch her program and set about making breakfast.

Homicide Division
Flagler Street
7:15 a.m.

Eva was used to the long days and nights the job called for, but Luis was still getting adjusted to life as a detective. They had spent most of the last seven-plus hours looking over missing persons reports and sending out a description of their "Jane Doe" to every law enforcement agency in the state.

Finally, the junior detective had gotten up and walked the three blocks to their favorite place for coffee and food, Bakery Pastelmania. A small gray building tucked up against a larger restaurant, it was heaven-to-go for the taste buds. Eva was sitting outside the front of the precinct as he returned with his hands full.

"Pastelito de Guayaba?"

"Yes, please." The pastry filled with sugary sweetness was one of her favorites.

After placing the treat into Eva's hand, he headed inside the precinct. "Coming?"

"In a minute."

She stepped into a shaded spot and pulled out her cell phone. Hitting the button to dial home, she listened to the ringing and waited. "Hola?"

"It's me, Mama."

"Good morning, dear."

"Is Maria getting off to Sunday School okay?"

"Yes, she's just running out the door. She sends her love."

"Tell her I love her, too."

"Will you be home for dinner?"

"Too soon to say, I'm afraid. I'll let you know if I can make it."

"No problem."

"Thanks, Mama."

Eva closed her phone and followed her partner back inside the precinct.

The Miami Police Department Headquarters was a large, two-story beige structure that sat catty-corner in the pie-shaped segment of land at Flagler and Twenty-Second Avenue. The front of the building was round and filled with windows to take in all of the odd intersection it inhabited. It had been designed to have a welcoming feel, which it did, but also to mask the ugly part of the business that went on behind its doors.

The Homicide Division was in the northern wing, on the second floor. The two detectives shared a cubicle, desks opposite each other across a small aisle that separated them. A steaming-hot cup of coffee was sitting on her desk when she got there.

She held it up and mouthed "thanks" to her partner, who was hanging up the phone as she sat down. "Autopsy is in an hour, if we want to go."

"Might as well. We're not accomplishing anything here."

"My thought exactly."

Apartment of
Rosie & Gabriela Torres
Fort Myers
7:45 a.m.

"It's ready, Mom. Can you make it to the table?"

Her show was over, so Rosie forced herself up and over to the small kitchenette. "Of course."

They sat together and Gabriela ate while her mother pushed her food around the plate. Gabby grinned at her mother, who looked up suspiciously. "What?"

"Nothing," Gabby laughed. "It's just I remember you telling me it wouldn't work to push my food around the plate, and I had to eat it."

Rosie smiled. "Yes. You always wanted dessert without eating dinner."

"It never worked, did it?"

"Not once! It never worked for me with my mama, either."

Rosie had traveled to the United States in nineteen-eighty, as part of the Mariel Boatlift, a mass exodus from Cuba orchestrated by Fidel Castro. She had only been four years old, and didn't remember much about the trip itself, but she loved to tell stories of their early days in Miami. Gabby braced herself for another rendition of one of the familiar tales, but her mother changed the subject instead. "You're a good cook, Gabriela."

"Thank you, Mama. But how would you know, you've barely touched your breakfast."

"I'm sorry, but I'm just not hungry."

Gabby was aware that one of two things was responsible when her mother was distracted like this. The first was the physical pain from the fall, which was always with Rosie, and the doctors said was made worse by a car accident she was in as a teen. The second was an emotional pain from the events surrounding that same car accident.

Nineteen at the time and engaged to Gabriela's father, she was riding in the back seat when her parents' car was hit head-on by a truck. Her mother and father died instantly, but a seatbelt and God's grace, saved Rosie. She spent a month and a half in the hospital, and even missed her parent's funeral, before finally being discharged.

Devastated and alone, Rosie married her fiancé shortly after getting out of the hospital. Ten months later, she gave birth to Gabriela. Four years of a bad marriage was enough, so Rosie divorced her husband and took her daughter to Fort Myers on the west coast of the state.

Gabby had never been sure which pain her mother treated with the heroin: the physical or the emotional. Probably both.

She cleared the plates and started another pot of coffee as Rosie got up and headed down the hall. "I think I'll lie down again."

"Okay. I will check on you in a little while."

Office of The Miami-Dade County Medical Examiner 10:00 a.m.

The coroner's domain was a rather non-descript, two-story structure connected to the sprawling downtown complex of Jackson Memorial Medical Center and the University of Miami Medical School. Located at One Bob Hope Road, the large campus included the Veteran's Hospital and the Holtz Children's Hospital.

Though they had attended many autopsies, Luis never got used to the smell. Eva, on the other hand, never seemed to notice. "Why the strange look, Luis?"

"You aren't bothered by the smell of this place?"

"What smell?"

He laughed. "Never mind."

They were standing behind in an observation room behind a thick pane of glass, watching Fuentes perform the post-mortem examination on their victim. The brightly lit autopsy room, filled with stainless steel and white linens, was always cold. Their vantage point was much more comfortable, but it meant they couldn't hear the doc as he was speaking.

The process was a familiar one. First, the body was photographed from head to toe, front to back. Then, using a large, circular magnifying glass at close range, every inch of the victim was closely inspected. Next, scrapings were extracted from fingernails and swabs taken from any skin abrasions or open wounds. Finally, samples were taken from every possible area that DNA or blood might be found. All of that came before the body was even opened up.

Eventually, the standard "Y" incision was made from each shoulder to the sternum, and down to the pelvic line. Every organ was removed, weighed, and had a sample taken to be put on a slide for microscopic examination. During the entire process, Fuentes recorded his thoughts into the overhanging microphone.

It was a painstaking process, and after nearly ninety minutes, the doc turned the body over to his associate. Looking toward them, he pointed to the double doors at the end of the room. Eva nodded and they walked out to meet the coroner.

Peeling off his gloves, he'd tossed them in a trash can, but was still wearing the white gown which showed the grim nature of his job. "Blunt force trauma."

Eva nodded. "Any idea of what was used?"

"Can't say for sure, but my hunch is a club or a piece of pipe. Whatever it was, she was struck multiple times about the face and head. There was considerable bleeding in the brain."

Luis had his notebook out. "What about the injuries to her back?"

"Older. They were in various stages of healing, so she definitely suffered multiple attacks over a long time, probably with the same weapon."

"How old?"

"Roughly eighteen to twenty-two."

Eva cursed under her breath. "Just a baby. Did you find any distinguishing marks?"

Fuentes nodded. "Small birthmark on the inside of the right thigh in a half-moon shape."

"What about sexual assault?"

He shook his head. "There was seminal fluid, and I'll have it tested, but she appeared to be active sexually. I wouldn't be surprised to find more than one DNA profile, and if I were you, I wouldn't want to rule out a tie to prostitution."

"Okay, Doc. Send the report up this afternoon?"

"Probably so."

Fuentes turned and went back through the double doors. Luis put away his notebook. "We need to add the birthmark to our statewide description."

"Yeah. Let's get out of here."

Monday, February 16

Apartment of
Rosie & Gabriela Torres
Fort Myers
8:45 a.m.

Gabby was running later than normal, but the extra money from working overtime would come in handy. She unlocked the door and set down a small bag of groceries. Rosie wasn't in the living room watching her soap and Gabby found herself fighting irritation at her mother not being out of bed yet.

"Mom!"

She put the milk in the fridge, and standing with the door open, listened for her mother's answer. Nothing.

"Mom?"

She waited another moment, then slammed the fridge door in frustration. Stomping to the bedroom door, she found it closed. When she pushed, it was stuck.

"Mama, answer me!"

The door gave slightly, so she leaned into it and got a crack big enough to push her head through. Lying on the floor against the back of the door was Rosie.

"Oh, no! Mama!"

Gabby leaned over and felt for a pulse but recoiled when she touched the cold of her mother's skin. Tears blurred her vision as she pushed the door farther open and ran to the phone.

"Lee County 9-1-1. What is your emergency?"

"My mother! She's on the bedroom floor and I think she's dead."

"Is she breathing?"

"No, and she's cold!"

As she sat on the side of the bed, her gaze fell on a needle at her feet, and the realization of what had happened flooded over her. *Heroin! Oh Mama, no!*

The emergency operator was still talking to her, but Gabriela had stopped listening. Her mother was dead, and she was too late. The phone fell to the floor, landing next to the needle as Gabby lay back on the bed, sobs wracking her very soul.

****

Sitting at the small kitchenette, Gabby watched as the blanket-covered gurney bearing her mother's body was rolled slowly out of the apartment. Rosie's form was hidden, including her face.

A detective was asking Gabby questions, mostly about her mother's drug habit. The police had found the needle, and like Gabby, had concluded it was an overdose. Nevertheless, they needed to make sure they covered all their bases. Without knowing she'd even answered any questions, the officer thanked her for her effort and closed his notepad.

An hour later, Gabby was still sitting in the same chair as the police prepared to leave. The detective stopped next to her. "Miss?"

"Yes."

"Are you going to be alright?"

She nodded without thinking about the question.

"Do you have any family we can call for you?"

That was the hardest part of all this. Gabby didn't have anyone. "No."

The detective set a card on the table. "That has the number to our Victim Center."

Gabby stared at it.

Is that what she was? A victim? Of what? Her mother's demons?

His voice was gentle. "They have a very good grief counseling unit."

Grief? Is that what this was? Or maybe this was shock and grief came later?

And then they were gone. She was alone.

She picked up her cell phone and looked through the contacts. There were only a few names, but finally she settled on her closest girlfriend at work, Sarah Potter. Somebody had to help her get through what had to be done in the next few days.

It rang several times and she was about to hang up when she heard the familiar voice. "Hello?"

"Sarah?"

"Yeah... Gabby? Is that you?"

"It's me..."

"What's wrong? You sound awful."

"Rosie is gone."

Momentary silence. "I'm so sorry, Gabby. Is there anything you need?"

"Actually, yes. Do you think you could..." She couldn't get the rest out before the tears came flooding back.

Sarah's voice came back strong. "I'm on my way."

Homicide Division
Flagler Street
9:15 a.m.

Eva had taken the opportunity to drop Maria off at school on her way to work. As a result, she wasn't there for the arrival of the fax, but Luis was waiting impatiently when she walked in. "We got a hit!"

"You're kidding? Already?"

"Sometimes you get lucky."

She set her coffee down on the desk and looked over her partner's shoulder at the sheet of paper. "Who is she?"

"Bonita Mendez, age twenty. She was reported missing by her family eighteen months ago."

"Have we got a positive ID?"

"The parents live up the coast in Palm Beach Gardens. I faxed some photos to a detective there, and the father identified her from them."

Eva closed her eyes, a subconscious reaction to the mental image of a father having to do one of the worst tasks she could imagine. Moving back to her own desk, she dropped into her chair. "Did you get an address for the parents?"

"Yeah. They're expecting us this afternoon. Also, the autopsy report came in after we left last night."

"Anything of use in it?"

"No. Pretty much everything was as Doc told us. There was no sand in her lungs, throat, or mouth, so death almost certainly occurred before arriving at the beach. He put her time of death between two and six hours before she was dumped."

"Palm Beach Gardens is maybe an hour and a half from here?"

"Sounds about right."

"Okay. We need to fill in the lieutenant, then we can head up there."

Luis looked at his watch. "Okay. I'll call the parents and let them know when we'll be there."

"Good. I'll brief the boss."

Home of Mr. & Mrs. Mendez Palm Beach Gardens 12:30 p.m.

The Mendez home was in a relatively new subdivision of Palm Beach Gardens, just northwest of Riviera Beach. Made up of stucco-covered, two-story structures that were multiple versions of themselves, the neighborhood's homes were different only in color. Coconut Palms shaded the quiet streets as they searched for the Mendez home.

Eva had driven the roughly eighty miles while Luis was giving directions. He was staring at the houses passing by, looking for the house number they were in search of, and was struck by the contrast between the autopsy the day before and the place they found themselves then.

"How does a girl, barely twenty years old, go from this place to the coroner's table in Miami?"

"I don't know, but I bet she had some help along the way."

Luis snorted. "Indeed." He pointed to his right. "There it is."

The Mendez's version of the stucco home was a pale yellow, equally tidy as the ones around it. Eva parked and climbed out into the warmth of the afternoon, grateful for the shade provided by multiple, tall palm trees on either side of the driveway. The two detectives approached the door, Luis pushing the lit button beside the entry. A sing-song doorbell belied the sadness they were about to find inside.

When the door finally opened, it slowly revealed a man no more than five feet tall, with curly hair that had turned completely white and a beard to match. His eyes were red from crying and his accent was heavily influenced by his Cuban heritage. "Hola."

"Señor Mendez?"

"Si."

Eva held up her badge. "My name is Detective Hernandez, and this is my partner, Detective Moreno."

"Yes. Please come in."

"Thank you."

The detectives followed the man down a dark hallway into a family room, itself equally dark. The house was eerily quiet, and to Eva's surprise, no one else was in the back room. "Is your wife here, Mr. Mendez?"

He shook his head. “She is with her sister making arrangements.”

“I see. I’m very sorry for your loss.”

“Thank you. Please sit. Some espresso, perhaps?”

Eva put her hand up to stop him. “We don’t want to be any trouble.”

“It is already made. Some for both of you?”

Eva smiled and Luis nodded, sending the little man off into the kitchen. As her eyes adjusted, the picture over the mantle at the end of the room came into view. She gestured at it, and her partner’s gaze followed her signal.

It was a large oil portrait of a girl about the same age as Eva’s daughter. She wore a bright yellow dress with a large bow at the waist, a wide smile, and dark hair that curled down her back almost to her waist. Luis shook his head sadly. “She was a beautiful girl.”

Eva fought to maintain control, easily able to see herself in the place of the Mendez family. She feared for her own Maria most every day, and despite her knowledge and precautions to watch over her, the detective and mother knew even her daughter was vulnerable to the darkness of the world.

When Mr. Mendez returned, he carried a tray holding a pot, three demitasse cups, and a plate of polvoróns. Luis accepted a cup and two of the Cuban sugar cookies. Eva accepted the same minus the cookies.

She pointed at the portrait. "Is that Bonita, sir?"

Mendez straightened himself and looked at the painting. "Si. She was ten years old when that was done." He turned back to the detective and apparently saw the pain on her face. "You have children, Detective?"

She nodded. "A daughter, Maria. She is eleven."

"They are God's gift. Unfortunately, our children are born with a will of their own, and we cannot control them for all their days, true?"

"True."

The man settled into the couch across from the detectives, sinking into the overstuffed piece of furniture until Eva thought he might disappear. Luis took out his notepad and laid it on the table, waiting for his partner to begin. She sipped her coffee, and finally accepted a cookie on the kind man's second offer.

Eventually, she pushed forward. "I know this must be very difficult, but I must ask you a few questions."

"Of course."

"When was the last time you saw your daughter?"

"It was in this very room, about a year and a half ago."

"What were the circumstances of that day?"

Mendez sighed. "She wanted to visit a friend in Little Havana. We didn't want to drive her so far away, and we didn't think it was safe for her to go alone. She became very angry."

"What happened?"

"After words with me, then her mother, she stormed out. She has... had her mother's temper." He forced a smile. "I assumed she would cool off and return later that night, but as you can see, she never did."

"Did you ever hear from her again?"

"Yes, about two days later. She called collect from a pay phone. Of course, we accepted the call and her mother begged her to come home. Bonita refused and wouldn't tell us where she was. She said she was fine and would be home in a few days."

The man stopped, obviously weary from recounting the story over and over again, mostly in his own mind. Eva let him catch his breath, watching as he sipped his espresso. He paused before the cup reached his lips. "I gave the phone number to the detectives when I reported her missing."

Eva and Luis exchanged hopeful glances. Eva set her cup down. "Do you still have the number?"

"Indeed. I still have the phone bill."

"May I see it?"

"Certainly." He rose and went down the hall, returning moments later with a piece of paper. When he handed it to Eva, she spotted the yellow highlighter, faded in the eighteen months since it was first marked. She read the number aloud to Luis, then the time and date of the call, which he noted. She returned the bill to Mr. Mendez.

Luis put away is notepad, stood, and reached out to shake hands with the man. "I'm very sorry for your loss, sir."

Mendez nodded. "Gracias."

Luis turned and headed to the door as Eva lagged behind. The man had not asked what his daughter was doing all the time she had been missing. "Are there any questions about your daughter that you would like answered?"

He forced a sad smile. "I don't know if you'll understand this, Miss Hernandez, but our daughter passed away in our hearts nearly a year and a half ago. We understood that wherever she was, she was probably dead, because she would have come home.

Whatever befell her, from the day we lost her until we got the call this morning, we do not want to know. It can only hurt us more."

He turned and pointed at the painting. "That is how we will remember our daughter until the day we see her again."

Eva wiped away the tears running down her cheeks. "Please give your wife my sympathies."

"I will, and thank you again."

Eva moved down the dark hallway, struggling to regain her composure, and at the door she stopped. When she turned, Mr. Mendez was watching her from the family room. "Mr. Mendez, do you want to know when we find who did this?"

He nodded slowly. "Si."

Tuesday, February 17

Southwest 6th Street
Little Havana
10:30 a.m.

Luis pulled his car off onto the side of the street in a parking spot directly across from the Cuban market. “That’s it.”

Eva studied the small convenience store on the end of a strip mall. It looked like the hundreds of others in the city: high windows covered by bars and a single entry door smothered in multiple layers of promo stickers. “It’s inside?”

“That’s what the phone company said.”

She opened her door. “Okay, let’s go.”

They stepped out into the noise of a frantic one-way street, pausing to judge the safest opening before dashing across the road. A set of wind chimes taped to the door jangled as they came into the store. The elderly woman behind the register, perched precariously on a stool, played with the bun of hair perched equally unbalanced on top of her head. Through a bobby pin she held between her teeth, she called out. "Buenos dias."

"Buenos dias," Eva flashed her badge. "My name is Detective Hernandez. Do you have a pay phone in here?"

"Si." She pointed with the pin she'd removed from her mouth. "Back there."

Luis went back to look at it while Eva pulled out a picture of Bonita Mendez. "Have you ever seen this girl?"

The elderly clerk took the picture, stared at it, then handed it back. "Maybe." She shrugged. "There are many girls that come in and out every day."

"But this one in particular?"

"She doesn't seem familiar."

Luis returned. "Nothing in the way of notes or things scrawled on the wall."

Eva nodded. "It was a long shot. Not many of those things left in use anymore."

They thanked the clerk for her time, then stepped outside. Luis looked down one way, then the other. Pulling his own photo of Bonita out, he smiled at his partner. "Which way do you want?"

Eva pointed to her right. "I'll go this way, meet you on the other side, back at the car."

"Works for me."

Apartment of Rosie & Gabriela Fort Myers 1:00 p.m.

Gabby was sitting on the bed in her mother's room, legs crossed under her, a shoebox of papers in front of her. It was hard to understand how her mother could live nearly forty years and have so little to show for it. A few photos, bunches of seemingly useless pieces of paper, and a few receipts. Even the furniture wasn't Rosie's, since the apartment had been furnished when they moved in.

Can this be all there is left?

She picked up one of the photos. Old and yellowed, it was of Gabby and her mom when Gabby was just a baby. Rosie's smile was wide and her eyes were full of life. If there was ever a moment her mother was happy, this had to be it, but that look had not returned in many years. In fact, Gabby couldn't remember the last time she had seen her mother truly happy.

She set the picture aside and looked at the next one. This one she had seen before, but only once. The day she had asked about her father. Rosie had gone into the bedroom and returned with the photo, handing it to Gabby.

"That's him."

Gabby had stared at it for a long time, as if he might say something to her, maybe tell her he loved her. "What was his name?"

Rosie was standing over her daughter, staring down at the photo in her hands. "Gabriel."

She looked up at her mother in surprise. "I was named after him?"

"That's right, and it was suitable that you were, too. You were the only thing good that ever came from that man."

"Do you know where his is?"

Rosie snorted. "I have no idea. He's probably dead by now."

Eventually, her mother took the picture back and disappeared into the bedroom.

Gabby touched the photo of his face, seeking some sort of a connection, but there was none. If her father was alive, she wouldn't know where to begin to look for him, or even if she would want to.

She was about to put everything back in the box when she spotted an envelope taped to the inside of the box. She pried at the Scotch tape with her fingernail and popped it loose. When she turned it over, she found it was addressed to her mother, and the postmark indicated it had been mailed from Miami.

Delicately, she removed a single, folded sheet of paper and a photo. Opening the note, she read the faded letter aloud.

Rosie,

You would probably like to have this photo of Mom and Dad with us.

I'll lose it anyway.

Javier

Gabby stared blankly at the note, her fingers shaking as she re-read it several times.

Mom and Dad? Rosie had a brother? Why had she never told me?

She turned the photo over and examined it. A black and white Polaroid of two adults and two children. They were standing on a dock, several fishing boats behind them, and a large crowd of people milling around. The man had his arms draped over the shoulders of a boy about six or seven years old, who was standing in front of him. The women had a little girl who couldn't have been more than four, standing in front of her. They all wore wide smiles as they stood in the bright sun.

It was easy to see the resemblance between the little girl and Rosie.

It has to be my grandmother and grandfather with Rosie, but who is the boy?

If the note was to be believed, his name was Javier, and he was what... Rosie's brother?

Gabby stuffed everything back in the shoebox except for the letter. Taking it and the picture to the living room, she stared at it in better light.

Rosie's maiden name was Estrada. That would make this boy, Javier Estrada. And to me, he would be Uncle Javier!

Gabby's mind reeled as she set the picture down to look at the envelope. The postmark date was just over six months old, and there was a return address.

The Castle Hotel
2100 SW 7th Street,
Miami, Fla. 33135

He could still be there. If he is, do I contact him? Maybe the reason Rosie never mentioned him was because he didn't want any contact with Rosie... or me.

Gabby wasn't certain her father was dead. It had occurred to her that Rosie said that to prevent Gabby from hunting for her father, but she could never know for sure now. However, if this Javier was still alive, he could be the only blood relative she had remaining.

She set the envelope aside and opened her laptop. Using Google Maps, she performed a search for the Castle Hotel. In seconds, she was looking at the location and a picture. Unfortunately, there was no man standing at the front door with an arrow indicating *This is Javier!* She smiled at her own silliness.

The map identified the address as being in Little Havana, but not much else. The photo was of a rather beat-up white stucco structure with malformed turrets, which no doubt had spawned the name of the place. The only real indications that it was a hotel and not an apartment building were the faded-yellow cloth cover over the front door and the peeling C-shaped sign declaring the name.

Not much to look at.

She scrolled the picture left, then right. The appearance of the place gave her the creeps. Using the Google feature allowing her to rotate the picture around, so she checked out the neighborhood. Several nicer-looking homes and apartment buildings were in the area, which was a little reassuring, but the hotel itself was still unsettling.

It's just a picture, Gabriela!

Below the address was a phone number. Impulsively, she picked up her phone and dialed it.

"Castle Hotel."

She snapped the phone shut.

What are you doing? Think about this. Do you want to speak with this man? What if he doesn't want to know you? He could be angry.

Gabby set her phone down and stared at the photo for a few minutes longer. Eventually, she closed the computer. She would wait at least until after the funeral, then decide what to do.

Southwest 6th Street
Little Havana
2:45 p.m.

Luis was waiting for her when Eva got back to the car. Doing neighborhood canvas is one of the least enjoyable parts of their job, but one of the most necessary. She climbed into the passenger seat, relishing the air conditioning which Luis had going full blast.

He handed her a cold bottle of water. “Here, you look like you could use this.”

“Thanks.”

“Any luck?”

She drank deeply before answering. “Nothing of any consequence. You?”

“Can’t say I did any better. Want to head back to the precinct?”

“Yeah. We’ll compare notes there.”

While his partner downed the last of her water, Luis pulled out into traffic and pointed them toward Flagler Street.

Wednesday, February 18

Fort Myers Cemetery
9:00 a.m.

Backing up against the City of Fort Myers Water Treatment plant, not far from the banks of the Caloosahatchee River, was the old Fort Myers Cemetery. It struck Gabby as an odd final resting place for a woman who, as a small child, had floated across the Straits of Florida. It was a perilous journey undertaken to a new homeland just to end up by a sewer plant.

Gabby was the only family present at the service, but several of the girls from work had come to support her, including Sarah. Though they weren't close, Gabby would never have gotten through all the planning or decisions without the kindness and strength her friend had supplied.

The day was warming nicely, and with little wind, the setting and ceremony were nice. Father Michaels from St. Francis Xavier Church was just finishing the service. He had met Rosie at the rehab center where he visited weekly.

"In our Lord's name, amen."

As the priest approached her, Gabby wiped at her eyes with the white kerchief she'd carried almost non-stop for the past two days. He reached out and laid a hand on her shoulder. "I'm so sorry, Gabriela."

"Thank you, Father. And thank you for such nice words today."

His smile was melancholy but warm. "She's no longer in pain; we can be thankful for that."

"True. It is some comfort."

"Addiction is a terrible thing. It's a controlling force none of us can understand if we've never faced it."

"I hope I never have to."

"Amen to that. Will you come see us at the church?"

"I'll try, Father. I don't know what I'm going to do, yet."

He hugged her and moved away, allowing Sarah to join Gabby for the walk back to the car. "Are you okay?"

"I guess... I'm just numb right now, you know?"

Sarah forced a smile. "Sounds like a normal reaction to me."

"Could you drop me at the apartment?"

"Of course. Would you like to stop for some lunch first?"

"That would be nice."

Homicide Division Flagler Street 9:30 a.m.

Eva groaned. "You ready to go over this stuff again?"

Luis nodded. "Yeah, I suppose."

"I feel the same, but right now, we've got nothing else."

"This stuff" was the interview notes they had each gathered the afternoon before. Despite spending several hours hashing them through the previous evening, they hadn't come up with a single name or place that triggered a new direction for their investigation. Eva had finally gone home an hour after Luis had called it a night.

She looked at the first page of her notes, then stopped. "Hey."

"What?"

"Why don't we trade off reading each other's notes out loud? Maybe it'll trigger something by hearing them in a different voice."

Luis shrugged. "Can't hurt."

They passed their notepads to each other and Eva stared at the first page of her partner's notes. "What is this? Latin?"

He laughed. "Just read!"

"Fine. Maesy Cafeteria—Dave Gomez—no ID on pic—too many girls come in to ID one."

Luis followed. "Raul's Auto Care—Interviewed owner, two mechanics—No ID on pic."

Eva read the next note. "Dollar Store—Armando Cardona, owner—no clerks—no ID—Too many female customers."

Luis followed up, and the reading continued back and forth for nearly an hour and a half. By the time they'd finished, Eva was hungry and doubly frustrated. "You want to get some lunch?"

Luis rubbed his eyes. "Yeah. Let's get out of here for a while."

"Agreed." She closed the notepad. "Here, take your chicken scratch back."

He grabbed it. "It's not chicken scratch, it's code."

Eva laughed. "If you say so!"

Apartment of
Rosie & Gabriela
Fort Myers
12:15 p.m.

Gabby sat staring at the picture of The Castle Hotel, doing her best to make a decision. She'd gone back and forth multiple times since yesterday, unable to bring herself to call, but equally unable to forget about the last possible connection to her mother, Uncle Javier.

If he was my uncle, and if he did want to speak to me, and if he wanted to know what happened to his sister, and if...

She could torture herself for days on end with the "ifs," but she would get no closer to an answer unless she called the number. So, more for her sanity than anything else, she picked up the phone and dialed.

It rang four or five times, and she was just about to chicken out when a voice came on the line. "Castle Hotel."

"Yes… um… I'm looking for Javier Estrada."

"He's not here."

"Okay. Do you think he will be there soon?"

"Depends."

The answer caught Gabby by surprise. "I'm sorry?"

"Who wants to know?"

"Oh. Well… I'm not sure he would know my name, but I'm calling about his sister."

"Sister? He ain't got no sister."

Gabby fought the urge to hang up. "Look, can you give him a message?"

"I guess."

"Tell him Gabriela called from Fort Myers with news about Rosie."

"Rosie?"

"Yes, Rosie Torres." She added her number to the message. "If he has any questions, he can call the number I just gave you."

"Okay, lady. I gotta run."

"Oh, that's fine. Thank…" There was a click in her ear. She set the phone down and tried to calm the pounding of her heart. Ten minutes later, she was still shaking.

Islas Canarias Restaurant
Little Havana
12:45 p.m.

Just ten minutes from the precinct, Islas Canarias was Eva's favorite spot to have lunch. Now that Luis was her partner, it had become one of his favorites as well. However, in his case, it was more by necessity than choice. Especially if his partner was going to buy.

"You having the usual?"

Eva smiled. "Of course."

The usual was carne asada, which Luis admitted was very good, but today he wanted something more like his mother's comfort food. He decided pot roast sounded good. "How's the ropa vieja?"

"Excellent."

"Sounds good to me."

The waitress arrived, took their orders, then disappeared.

Islas Canarias had everything from breakfast through dinner, all of it homemade. White tablecloths covered square tables sporting white cloth napkins. The bland table settings were in direct contrast to the bright colors of the Spanish-influenced mural across the entire back wall. Bright reds, yellows, pinks, and blues formed a large street musician scene.

Luis sipped his coffee, noticing his partner seemed distracted. “Something wrong, Eva?”

She furrowed her brow. “I’m not sure. Do you have your notepad?”

“Sure.” He retrieved it from his back pocket. “Why?”

“Go through each of the interviews and tell me the reason they gave for not being able to ID our girl’s picture.”

“Um… Okay.” He opened the pad and went from one page to the next. “Many girl customers—too many girls to know for sure—many girls’ faces…”

Their food arrived. He waited until the food was set in front of them and the server was gone before continuing. “Many… That’s odd.”

Eva was nodding at him. “Think about the area. It’s divided by a main thoroughfare and is mostly industrial, with some retirement apartments.”

“Yeah, so why is ‘many girls’ the main excuse? Is it a busy area for prostitution?”

“I had the exact same question. I didn’t see any hookers when we were there, did you?”

Luis shook his head. "Not that I can remember."

"Even being the middle of the day, some should have been out if that is an active area. Let's eat and after lunch we can check in with Vice. Then, depending on what they have to say, maybe we'll run back out to the neighborhood. We need to find out where all these girls are coming from, or if they even exist."

Apartment of Rosie & Gabriela Fort Myers 1:30 p.m.

Gabby hadn't exactly been watching her phone, but when it did ring, she stared at it as if it might explode. Moving toward where it sat on the coffee table, she peered at the number on the caller ID. The area code was 305.

Miami. It's him.

Summoning her courage, she opened her phone. "Hello?"

"Gabriela?"

"Yes."

"I am returning your call. This is your Uncle Javier."

He called himself my uncle!

"Hi. I didn't know if you knew who I was."

He laughed. "Oh yes, I know you. It is you who does not know me."

He sounds... nice.

"I… I confess, until yesterday, I had never even heard your name."

"I know. Rosie and I have not been close all these years. There are things we don't agree upon and never have."

"I see…" She didn't.

"Your message said there was news about my sister."

Suddenly, the real reason for the phone call came crashing in. "Oh, um… yes."

"Is she listening in? Does she not approve of you calling me?"

"No… she's… Rosie's gone."

"Gone?"

"She died a few days ago."

"Oh," There was a long pause. "That is too bad. How did she die?"

The realization she hadn't thought this conversation through came washing over Gabby.

How do you tell a complete stranger his sister died from a heroin overdose?

"Was it the drugs?"

Gabby was caught off guard.

How could he know about her habit?

"Yes."

"I am sorry to say it, but I am not surprised. Has the funeral been held?"

"It was this morning."

"I am sorry I missed it. How are you doing? Are you okay?"

This entire conversation had turned her world upside down. She found herself needing to sit down.

Could Rosie have been in touch with her brother all these years? Why would she have kept him a secret?

"Gabriela?"

She fought to steady herself. "Yes, I'm here. It's been a difficult few days, but I'll be okay."

"Good. I must run, but may I call in the next day or so? I'd like to know more about you."

"Of course. I would like that."

"Very well. Goodbye."

The line went dead and Gabby laid the phone down. The picture of the family on the dock looked back at her from the coffee table. She found herself staring at the little boy, entranced by his smile coming back at her from a time many years before.

Finally, she lay down on the couch and shut her eyes. The world had started spinning and was picking up speed.

Parking Lot
Islas Canarias Restaurant
Little Havana
1:45 p.m.

The phone rang just once before someone picked up. "Miami Vice Squad."

"Jack?"

"Yeah, who's this?"

"Eva, Eva Hernandez."

"Eva! Long time. How are you?"

"Good. You?"

"Same ol' and then some. How's Maria?"

Eva smiled at the mention of her daughter. "Getting bigger every day."

"Glad to hear it. Tell her I said hi."

"I will."

"So, to what do I owe the call?"

"I need information on some possible prostitution activity."

"You're not getting into a new line of work, are you?"

"Not yet!" Eva laughed. "Actually, my partner and I were canvassing a neighborhood yesterday and were told there were a lot of girls coming into the businesses. We wondered if you guys were working the area?"

"Where about?"

"Southwest Sixth Street, say from Twelfth to Seventeenth Avenue?"

"Nooo… hold on." Jack came back in less than two minutes. "Nothing shows up in the reports. Most of our focus these days is in the area around the airport and on South Beach."

"Okay, Jack. Thanks."

"Any time."

Eva hung up. "Nothing from Vice, so let's go see what we can dig up."

Luis started the car. "Sounds like a plan."

****

An hour and a half later, Eva was interviewing the fourth name on her list and still had gotten nothing more from the shop owners than the last time she'd been there.

Frustrated, she was headed back to the car when her phone rang. "Hey."

It was Luis. "Where are you?"

"At the corner of Seventeenth and Sixth. Why?"

"You know the dollar store where I did a previous interview?"

"Yeah."

"Come down here."

"Okay. Give me five minutes."

When she came through the door, a nervous-looking man was chatting with a smiling Luis. Her partner waved for Eva to join him at the counter. "Armando, this is Detective Hernandez."

Armando forced a smile, glancing toward the door. "Buenos dias."

Eva nodded. "Buenos dias."

Luis gestured toward the man with his thumb. "Armando here, the owner of this establishment, was just telling me about a place called… What was that name again?"

"The Castle Hotel."

"That's right! The Castle Hotel over on Seventh Street, just a few blocks from here."

Eva played along. "Really? Nice place?"

Luis shook his head. "Not according to Armando." He looked at the man. "Tell her what you told me, Armando."

Eva could tell Armando was not happy talking about the current subject, and when he hesitated, she tried her most soothing tone. “Please, Armando. If you know something, you could be saving lives.”

“Okay, but no names. You didn’t hear this from me, understand?”

“Strictly confidential, you have my word.”

Another brief hesitation. “There’s girls who come in here on occasion, some of them have bruises.”

The detectives exchanged glances. Eva coaxed Armando to continue. “Did you ask them about the bruises?”

“No, I couldn’t.”

“Why not?”

“There’s always somebody with them.”

“Somebody?”

“A guy.”

The bell on the door jangled and a man came into the store. He waved at Armando, went to the back for some beer, then came to the register. The detectives stepped aside as Armando smiled uncomfortably. “Buenos dias, Roberto.”

“Buenos dias.”

“Do you want a sack?”

“Si.”

Armando bagged the beer, gave Roberto his change, and the man left. Eva came back to the counter. "You were telling me about this guy who's with the girls."

"Yeah. He almost never talks but stays close to them. Usually, the girls are getting personal items, if you know what I mean, and they seem to be afraid of him."

"Can you describe this man?"

"Big with his head shaved bald, but otherwise nothing special."

"Would you be able to ID him if you saw him again?"

"Sure."

Luis put away his notepad. "Tell my partner how you learned about the Castle Hotel."

Armando checked the door again. "The only time he ever said anything to me was when he gave me that business card."

Luis produced the card and held it up. "What did he say when he gave you this?"

"It was creepy. He said if I ever get lonely and need some comfort, stop by the hotel."

Eva pulled out her own business card. "If that man comes in here, will you give us a call?"

"I'll try, but I have the definite sense this guy is not someone to piss off, you know what I mean?"

Eva nodded. “I do. Don’t endanger yourself in any way, but we’d like to know if you see him again. Okay?”

Armando took the card and slipped it under the cash drawer. “Okay, but no guarantees.”

“Fair enough.”

The door chimed again and the detectives made their exit. Back at the car, Eva checked the address on her phone. “It’s a block over and two more east.”

Luis put the car in drive and turned left. Two minutes later, they were parked outside the Castle Hotel. Luis wasn’t impressed. “Not much to look at.”

Eva’s face reflected the concern she felt. “That’s what bothers me. Who knows what goes on inside those walls.”

They got out and walked under the tattered yellow entrance canvas into the office. Nobody was at the desk, but a rusted bell was sitting next to a sign that read “ring for service,” which Luis did. The furniture was cheap vinyl in turquoise and brown, torn from neglect, and the windows were grimy from street dirt.

“Can I help you?”

The question came from a partially open door that led from behind the desk to a back office. The voice belonged to a young man who easily matched the clerk’s description of "big and bald." Luis had his badge out. "Detective Moreno. This is my partner, Detective Hernandez."

The man stepped into the desk area and shut the door behind him. "Is there a problem?"

"Are you the owner?"

"No. I'm the manager."

"What's your name?"

"Rafael Castro."

Eva took out her notepad and wrote it down. "What is the room rate here, Rafael?"

"Depends."

Eva arched an eyebrow. "Oh? On what?"

"If you want a night, a week, or a month."

"I see. So the Castle Hotel is more of a rooming house?"

The big man shifted uncomfortably. "I guess."

"Would it be alright if we took a look around?"

"I can't allow that."

Luis leaned on the counter, getting very close to the manager. "Really? Why is that?"

"My boss has a strict rule about non-renters wandering around the complex."

"Oh, well then, let's see if we can convince *him* to let us check things out."

"He's not here."

"Where is he?"

"Out of town until tomorrow."

Eva was about to close her notepad, but stopped. "Is your boss the owner?"

"Yes."

"And what is his name?"

"Javier Estrada."

Thursday, February 19

Salvation Army Thrift Store
Fort Myers
8:15 a.m.

Gabby loaded the last of the bags into the cart and pushed it into the donation center. Sarah waited in the car as the last of Rosie's belongings were made available for other folks to buy. Gabby had considered a yard sale, but the idea of watching people pick over her mother's few remaining items seemed too difficult, even cold.

After the volunteer accepted the donation, Gabby walked back out and climbed into Sarah's car. "I feel good about doing that."

Sarah smiled. "You should."

"Thanks again for bringing me. There's a secondhand store near the apartment, but Rosie liked to shop at the Salvation Army, so it seemed more fitting."

Sarah pulled out into traffic. "What are you going to do now?"

"I don't know. Do you want to get some coffee?"

"Sure, but I meant as far as long term. Can you keep the apartment?"

"I can afford it, I've been paying most of the bills anyway, but I'm not sure I want to."

"Have you considered getting a clean start in a new place?"

"You mean a different city?"

Sarah laughed. "No, not quite so big. I was wondering if you might want to share an apartment. I need to get out of my place and I thought we might room together."

For the first time in several days, a real smile split Gabby's face. "Oh Sarah, I think that's a great idea. Are you sure?"

"Yeah. I think we'd be great roommates!"

"Then it's a plan."

Sarah pulled into a Starbucks. "Celebrate over frappuccinos?"

"Perfect."

Castle Hotel
Little Havana
9:15 a.m.

When the detectives arrived back at the Castle Hotel the next morning, they were met by the same empty office as the first time, but the person responding to the bell was somebody new. "What can I do for you?"

Eva held up her badge. "I'm Detective Hernandez with Miami PD, and this is Detective Moreno. Are you Javier Estrada?"

"My manager told me you had come by. Is there a problem?"

Luis instantly disliked Estrada. "My partner asked you a question."

Estrada sized up Luis, then turned back to Eva. "Yes, I'm Javier Estrada."

Eva had the same reaction as her partner. "How would you classify your little establishment here?"

"What do you mean?"

"Well, you can't really be considered a hotel, can you?"

"Not in the typical sense, I suppose. But we do rent rooms on a short-term basis to a wide range of guests."

"I see. Well, my partner and I would like to take a look around, maybe speak to some of your guests."

"I don't think that will be possible."

Luis stepped a little closer to the man, but Estrada stood his ground, staring directly at the detective. Luis pushed the issue. "Why would that be a problem?"

"My guests appreciate their privacy."

"We can get a warrant."

"Oh, really? Based on what?"

"Suspicion of murder."

Estrada wasn't impressed by the detective's tactic. "Murder? I'm shocked. How could you possibly have tied my humble establishment to such a heinous crime?"

Well aware they were in no position to get a warrant, Eva could see Estrada knew the same thing. She decided to pull back and wait for another opportunity. "Come on, Luis. Clearly, Mr. Estrada has other things he'd rather be doing."

"As a matter of fact, I do. I was just getting ready to make an important business call when you came in. Will that be all, detectives?"

"That's all." Eva moved to the door. "For now."

Back outside, Luis said out loud what they both were thinking. "That's a cool customer, and he's not someone I'd want to be on the wrong side of."

"Agreed. Let's get back to the precinct."

Apartment of Gabriela
Fort Myers
10:00 a.m.

Back at the apartment, Gabby was making herself a snack when her phone rang. She answered without looking at the caller ID.

"Hello?"

"Gabriela?"

"Yes. Who is this?"

"Uncle Javier."

"Oh… hi. I wasn't expecting to hear from you. How are you?"

"Bueno! How are you getting along?"

"Oh, okay I guess."

"Is this a bad time to have called?"

His concern for her seemed genuine and it touched her. "No… no, it's fine."

"Good, because I wanted to speak to you about your plans."

"My plans?"

"Yes. With your mother gone, do you have an idea what you're going to do now?"

Gabby was surprised. "Oh… well, I have my job."

Javier laughed. "Of course you do. I am being silly. What I'm trying to say is I have a suggestion for you if you would be interested."

"A suggestion?"

"Yes. As you know, I have the hotel here in Miami, and I could use some help. If you wanted to move down here, I could give you a position."

The idea caught Gabby completely off guard. She had struggled just to get the nerve up to call him, and now he was offering to give her a fresh start in Miami. At first blush, the idea appealed to her. Then she thought of Sarah. *I just promised to room with her!*

"Gabriela? Are you there?"

"Yes… oh, yes. I'm sorry. It's just your offer comes as a surprise."

Concern for her again crept into his voice. "No, it is me who is sorry. I am estúpido! Obviously, you need time to gather yourself after such a sad event."

"Oh, please don't take offence. Your offer is very kind, but I need to consider several things before I could say yes or no."

"Of course. My offer is genuine and it is ready when you are, because you are family."

Gabby nearly burst into tears at the word *family*. Immediately after the death of Rosie, she had felt completely alone, adrift in an emotional sea, with no port to come home to. Just the fact that someone could call her family filled a void inside her, at least partially.

"Thank you. I will consider it, I promise."

"Bueno! I must go, but I will talk to you soon, no?"

"Of course."

Gabby set her phone down, her face bearing a big smile. *Things are looking up!*

Homicide Division
Flagler Street
1:15 p.m.

Eva sat down at her computer after lunch, typed in the name Javier Estrada, and pushed *Search.* Within minutes, she had several dozen files matching the name in the Miami metro criminal database. A quick count showed thirty-four, so she started with birthdates, eliminating all that were obviously too old or too young.

This narrowed the field down to eleven. One by one, she pulled up the mug shots, until Estrada number seven was staring at her. "I found him."

Luis came around and peered over her shoulder. "That's him alright. Print it and I'll go fetch."

Eva hit the button, and five minutes later, they were poring over Javier Renaldo Estrada's file. Eva was studying a crime report while Luis read the arrest record aloud.

"He's been arrested thirteen times, charged six times, and served two sentences. One for assault with a deadly weapon, and one for attempted murder. He got off parole eight months ago."

Eva handed the piece of paper she was reading to Luis. "That report was filed by a young woman who claimed he beat her up when she wouldn't perform for him sexually."

"He's a real peach."

"You said he was on parole until recently?"

"Yeah."

"Who was his parole officer?"

Luis rifled through the sheets again. “Jerry Carson.”

Eva picked up her phone and dialed the Miami-Dade Parole and Probation Office. “Jerry Carson, please.”

She waited a few seconds, then left a message. “Yes Jerry, this is Detective Eva Hernandez. I have a question about one of your former parolees. Could you call when you get in tomorrow? Thanks.”

She hung up. “He’s out for the remainder of the day.”

Luis grinned at her. “There’s a lot more reading material here. I say we need some coffee?”

“You, sir, are a genius.”

Apartment of
Sarah Potter
Fort Myers
5:30 p.m.

Sarah and Gabby arrived back at Sarah’s with their arms full of groceries. As Gabby propped herself on a stool, Sarah began putting everything away. “Thanks for going with me.”

Gabby dismissed her with a wave. "Are you kidding? I was glad you called."

"What do you want to eat?"

"I don't care. What about that frozen pizza you just put away?"

Sarah retrieved it from the freezer. "Good idea. And I've got a bottle of red wine, so we can eat like princesses!"

"Great! Where's the wine?"

Sarah pointed at a cabinet. "In there."

"And the wine cork remover thing?"

Sarah laughed. "You mean the corkscrew?"

Gabby grinned at her. "That's what I said. The wine cork remover thing!"

"In that drawer, and the glasses are up there."

Gabby gathered everything together, and by the time the wine glasses were filled, Sarah had the pizza in the oven.

Sarah held up her glass. "To more nights like this as roomies!"

Gabby reluctantly clinked her glass with her own. "Yeah, about that."

"Did you change your mind?"

"No… not exactly. I still think we'd be great roommates, but something else has come up."

Sarah sipped her wine, disappointment etching her face. "Oh?"

"Yeah. I spoke with an uncle I didn't know I had."

"You're kidding?"

"No, I'm serious. Crazy, huh?"

"What does he want? Is he going to move in with you?"

"No!" Gabby set her glass down on the table. "Wait, let me back up and start from the beginning."

"Okay."

"I was going through Rosie's stuff when I found a photograph and letter that mentioned a man named Javier. So, I did a little detective work and found him in Miami."

"Look at you going all Sherlock Holmes!"

Gabby smiled. "I know, right! Anyway, I called him and we ended up talking. He's Rosie's brother."

"No way! Rosie never mentioned him?"

Gabby shook her head. "Not once."

"So, what happened when you talked?"

"Nothing much until this morning. He called and offered me a chance to start over in Miami."

"Start over?"

"Yeah. A job and a place to stay. I guess he was thinking I might want to be near family or something."

"Wow!" Sarah refilled their wine glasses. "That's pretty cool."

Gabby was surprised. "You think so?"

"Yeah. Miami is great."

"You've been?"

"Once, a few years ago. I loved it."

"So, you think I should go? I'd feel terrible for abandoning you after we made plans."

"Nonsense. Sure, you may ruin the rest of my life, but hey, you got to do what you got to do!" Sarah's smile gave her away. "Seriously, it's worth considering, for sure. If it were me, I'd probably jump at the chance."

"Really? You'd go?"

"Sure, why not? It'd be a big adventure."

Gabby snapped her fingers. "That's a great idea!"

Sarah laughed. "Thanks. What are you talking about?"

"Why don't you go with me?"

Sarah sat forward and set down her own glass. "Oh, I don't know. This is a family thing you have going on. Your uncle doesn't want me tagging along."

"How do you know?"

Sarah shrugged.

Gabby’s face was lit up now with the idea. “I can ask. Would you go if it worked out?”

“Sure.”

Gabby picked up her wine glass. “To rooming in Miami!”

Sarah grabbed her own and clinked it with Gabby’s. “To Rooming in Miami!”

Friday, February 20

Home of
Detective Eva Hernandez
Little Havana
8:15 a.m.

"Maria! Are you ready?"

"Yes, Momma."

Her daughter came skipping out of her bedroom, her black, wavy hair flowing behind her and a big smile on her face. Eva took Maria to school whenever she could. The girl, now beginning to show the first signs of becoming a teen, stopped in front of her. Tanned, with big brown eyes and a tiny nose, she had an undeniable charm.

"How do I look?"

Eva touched her chin. "You look wonderful."

"Thanks."

Eva grabbed her purse and headed for the door. "Let's go."

They were just a few minutes from the school when her phone rang. "This is Detective Hernandez."

"Good morning. This is Jerry Carson. I'm returning your call."

"Oh yes, good morning. I called because I'm interested in a parolee you handled last year."

"What's his name?"

"Javier Estrada."

"What has Mr. Estrada gotten himself involved in now?"

Eva turned the car into the drop-off area at the school. "Would you hold on a second, Jerry?"

"Of course."

Maria undid her seatbelt and leaned across to kiss Eva on the cheek. Eva covered the phone. "Have a good day, sweetie."

"I will Momma. Bye."

When the door was closed, Eva pulled into traffic and went back to her call. "Jerry?"

"Still here."

"Thanks, I was dropping off my daughter. Right now, I don't have anything particular on Estrada, but his name has come up in a murder investigation, and I'm looking for background on him."

"What kind of background?"

"Well, I've met him once, and he struck me as cool under pressure."

Jerry laughed. "That's for sure. I've never seen him out of control, but I'll say this, it's likely not a pretty sight. He's been charged with multiple vicious beatings, but only faced trial a couple times."

"Why were the charges dismissed in the other cases?"

"The women refused to testify."

"All his victims were women?"

"Except the attempted murder conviction. That was a male associate of his. Have you seen any of his victims' photos?"

"No, not yet."

"The guy's an animal, but he's not stupid. Estrada is the classic 'wolf in sheep's clothing' type. He can apparently be completely charming to the women he entraps, to the point they never see it coming."

"I didn't see anything related to prostitution. Is he involved with that?"

"Not that I'm aware of, but it would certainly fit his character."

Eva was just pulling into the precinct. "Okay, Jerry. Thanks a bunch."

"Anytime. Bye."

She closed her phone.

Time to pull the case files. This should be fun.

Apartment of Gabriela
Fort Myers
8:00 a.m.

Gabby finished putting her makeup on, then checked the time. She had been moved to the day shift and still had an hour before she had to be at work, so she dialed her uncle's number. It rang several times before he picked up. "Hello?"

"Uncle Javier? It's Gabriela."

"Gabriela! How nice to hear from you."

"You aren't busy, are you?"

"I'm never too busy to talk to you."

She smiled. "You know the idea we discussed yesterday?"

"Yes, of course."

"Well, I was thinking I might like to take you up on it."

"Wonderful! I'd be glad to have you here."

"But, there's something else."

"Oh?"

"I have a friend here in town who has helped me through the last week or so, and well, I promised I would room with her."

"I see. You don't want to break your promise, is that it?"

"I kinda feel bad."

His tone became serious. "It is very honorable of you to feel that way. Your mother would be proud. Tell me about this friend."

"Well, her name is Sarah. She works with me and has no family here, either. When I told her I was thinking about moving to Miami, she said it sounded great. So, that's why I called. Would it be a problem if she came with me?"

He laughed. "A problem? I think not. If she is a friend of yours, then she is welcome in my home. I may even be able to find her a position at the hotel, too."

"Oh, Uncle Javier, that would be wonderful!"

"When will you come?"

Gabby hadn't gotten that far in her thought process. "I'm not sure. I need to talk with Sarah and call you back."

"Very good. Talk to you soon then."

"Okay, and thanks again."

"I'm glad to do it. Bye."

Gabby hung up and dialed Sarah. "You've reached Sarah's phone. Leave your name and number after the beep and I'll call you back."

Gabby hung up without leaving a message. *Sarah must be at work already. This is too good to tell her on a voicemail.*

She grabbed her purse and rushed out the door.

Homicide Division Flagler Street 9:15 a.m.

"Here they are." Luis laid the files on the conference table in front of his partner. "These are the two conviction files and the four dropped charges. Where do you want to start?"

Eva slid the top folder toward her. "I'll take the first file. You start on the second and we'll make our way through."

"Works for me."

Eva flipped open her file. The top page was a summary of the judge's sentence. The second was the jury's decision, and the third listed the initial charges. She had grabbed the attempted murder file. At the back of the folder were the photos Jerry Carson had mentioned. He was right, they were gruesome.

A Hispanic man in his late twenties had been beaten by a piece of pipe. Both eye sockets were crushed and his nose broken by multiple blows about the head. A similar set of pictures were taken of the victim's torso, both front and back, revealing bruises everywhere.

Man, Estrada clearly meant to kill this guy!

Luis was across from her, shaking his head. "Have you got photos in your file?"

She nodded. "Ugly stuff."

"You can say that again. I've got the assault with a deadly weapon file, and this girl is unrecognizable."

"Does it say what he used on her?"

Her partner lifted a page. "A piece of pipe."

"I've got the attempted murder file. He used the same weapon here, and the pictures are the same as what you're looking at."

Eva closed her file and grabbed the next one, a thin folder with only three sheets inside. Luis mimicked her and they read in silence for several minutes. Finally, Luis moved on to another file, but Eva was intrigued by hers. The victim was a girl who matched their murder victim in almost every way, and the case was just four months old, meaning it happened after Estrada got off parole.

Eighteen, brown hair, Hispanic, older bruises on back and buttocks, beaten around the head. The key difference was she survived. Eva checked the name and address.

Veronica Borrego, age twenty-one, reported missing from Naples three months before the attack. No charges filed.

There was a phone number listed on the victim's information sheet. Eva dialed it as Luis finished with another file. "Who are you calling?"

Eva slid the folder toward him. "This is one of the girls who never filed charges. I was thinking we might go talk to her."

An elderly voice answered. "Hello?"

"Yes, is Veronica Borrego there, please?"

"May I ask who's calling?"

"My name is Detective Hernandez with the Miami Police Department."

"She is not here at the moment, Detective. I am her grandmother. May I ask what this is about?"

"I'd like to speak to her about the attack she suffered four months ago."

"My granddaughter has made her feelings very clear on that. She does not wish to press charges."

"I understand, ma'am. I am not investigating her case, but I am trying to solve an attack on another girl who was not as fortunate as your granddaughter. I was hoping to get some information from Veronica."

There was a hesitation on the other end. "Veronica will be home this afternoon, if you wish to call back."

"Actually, would it be okay if we came and saw her in person?"

Another pause. "I suppose."

"Thank you, ma'am. We will be there this afternoon. Goodbye."

Luis was watching her when she hung up. "So? Road trip?"

"That's right. I'll tell the lieutenant."

Denny's Restaurant
Fort Myers
10:45 a.m.

Gabby worked at the same restaurant as her mother. Sarah had replaced Rosie after the accident. There was finally a lull between the breakfast and lunch crowds. Gabby pulled Sarah aside and gave her the news. "I talked to my uncle."

"And?"

"He said you were welcome to come along. He even said he might have a position for you at his hotel!"

"You're kidding!"

"Nope. What do you say? Are we going to Miami?"

"Yeah! Roomies in Miami!"

Gabby laughed, giddy with excitement. "Roomies in Miami!"

"We need to make plans. You want to come over to my place after work?"

"Perfect."

The manager, who saw himself as a sort of ruler over the restaurant, signaled Sarah from across the dining room. "Attila the Hun is waving at me. I've got a table."

"Just think, pretty soon we can give notice and be free from his tyranny!"

Sarah laughed. "The sooner the better!"

Home of Veronica Borrego Naples 2:30 p.m.

The trip across the Everglades took just over two hours. Residents called the old two-lane stretch to Naples Alligator Alley, but the new I-75 had been named the Everglades Parkway. It cut the travel time across the state significantly, and it sounded less threatening to the tourists.

Veronica Borrego lived in the Palm Lake Mobile Home Park with her grandmother. The 1970's trailer was beige and green, neatly kept, but small.

Eva parked the car and the detectives approached the door. A covered porch shaded them as they knocked and waited. Shortly, the door opened a crack and an elderly woman peered at them. "Yes?"

Eva showed her badge. "My name is Detective Hernandez. I called earlier this morning."

The door opened completely. "Hello. I am Sylvia. Please come in."

Following Sylvia through the door and into a cramped living room, Eva surmised the furniture was the same age as the trailer. The air conditioning was not running and the interior was stuffy.

Sylvia gestured toward the couch. “Please, sit. I will get Veronica.”

Eva lowered herself onto the couch, but Luis opted to stay by the door. A few moments later, a young woman appeared without her grandmother. “Hi.”

Eva was surprised. “Are you Veronica?”

“Yes.”

The girl in front of the detectives was heavier, by at least forty pounds over the picture they’d seen, and had short, bleach-blonde hair. Her smile was hesitant. “I look different than you expected, don’t I?”

“Well, frankly, yes.”

“It’s on purpose. I want to make sure Javier never finds me again.”

She wore gray sweatpants and a red t-shirt. Her face was devoid of makeup and Eva’s heart broke at the effects of the trauma this poor girl had gone through. “Do you mind sitting with me?”

Veronica moved to the chair opposite Eva. When she was seated, Eva held out her hand. “I’m Eva.”

The girl shook the detective’s hand cautiously. “Ronnie.”

"I appreciate you agreeing to talk with us."

"Grandma said you're working on another girl's death."

"That's right."

"Did Javier kill her?"

Eva shrugged. "I don't know, but I intend to find out."

"I would have tried to stop him, but I was too afraid. He would have killed me, I know it."

Eva touched the girl's hand. "Nobody is suggesting otherwise. What you went through was horrific, and most people wouldn't have survived."

Ronnie's eyes welled up, but she kept her composure. "What do you need from me?"

"Could you tell me what happened?"

Ronnie's gaze went to Luis, then back to Eva. The female detective recognized the look immediately. "Luis, could you give us a few minutes?"

"Absolutely. I need to make a call, anyway."

"Thanks." Eva waited until her partner had stepped outside, then turned back to Ronnie. "Okay, go ahead."

The girl physically drew herself up, like taking a big breath to blow out candles, before starting.

"I was living with him because I had no place to go. I'd run away from here and hitched to Miami. He saw me in a convenience store and offered me a place to stay. He was very friendly, even warm, and I wasn't afraid. He fed me, put me up in his home, and told me I could stay as long as I needed."

"Did he ever make advances toward you?"

Ronnie shook her head. "Not once. He was a perfect gentleman."

"How long did you stay with him?"

"About two months. Then one day, he came home with another man. I didn't recognize him, but Javier took me into the back bedroom and told me I had to have sex with his guest."

Eva's stomach began to tighten, the routine a familiar one. "What happened next?"

"I told him no way! I'm no whore. He said I owed him for taking care of me, and I would do as I was told. When I told him he was crazy, he slapped me."

"Was that the first time he ever hit you?"

"Yeah. Suddenly, I was looking into the eyes of a lunatic. I didn't know who he was. I mean… he physically changed. He became angry, hateful, cruel."

Eva could feel the flushing of her face as the anger began to build. Ronnie shook as she relived it, hesitating, but Eva needed the rest of the story. “It’s okay, Ronnie. You’re safe here. Go ahead.”

“Well, I tried to get to the door, but he grabbed my hair and yanked me back. He started hitting me with his fist until I was nearly unconscious. Eventually, he left the room. I don’t know if he was going to come back or get the man, but I didn’t want to find out. I forced myself to crawl over by the window and stand. Once the window was open, I pushed myself through the screen and fell into the yard. I tried to get up and run but didn’t have the strength. Finally, I just laid there and screamed for help.”

“Did a neighbor call police?”

“I guess, but Javier came and got me before they arrived. He dragged me back into the house and hit me some more.”

Tears were streaming down the girl’s face now.

“Eventually, the police came to the door. When they insisted on speaking to me, Javier came and got me from the back bedroom. Before taking me to the door, he grabbed my face between his hands and said if I blamed him, he would kill me.”

“Is that why you didn’t press charges?”

Ronnie nodded.

"What happened when you got to the front door?"

"The officers asked me what happened and I told them I fell."

"Did they believe you?"

"I don't think so. Anyway, when they asked if they could call an ambulance, I said yes. That's how I got to the hospital."

"Were you questioned at the hospital?"

"Yes, but I stuck to my story. I just wanted them to call my grandmother. She came and got me."

Eva moved around the coffee table and wrapped Ronnie in her arms as the girl started to sob uncontrollably. For nearly ten minutes, she held her. Eventually, Ronnie composed herself. "Thank you."

Eva smiled, wiping the tears from Ronnie's cheeks. "You were very brave. You should be proud of yourself."

Ronnie gave her a weak smile.

Eva had one more question. "Ronnie, did he ever mention a hotel to you?"

The girl looked confused. "No. Why?"

"Nothing. Just a question."

Almost on cue, Sylvia appeared from somewhere in the back. Eva stood and moved to the door. "Thank you very much. Both of you."

She stepped outside to find Luis sitting on the porch in a swing. "How did it go?"

"It was rough. I'll tell you on the drive back to Miami."

Apartment of
Sarah Potter
Fort Myers
6:30 p.m.

"Uncle Javier?"

"Yes?"

"It's Gabriela."

"Yes, dear. Did you speak with your friend?"

"I did. She's here with me now."

"And what did you two young ladies decide?"

"We're moving to Miami!"

"Fabulous! I look forward to seeing you soon."

"We're just discussing our plans, so I'll let you know when we have a timeline, if that's okay."

"Okay? It's better than okay, it's great. My home is ready when you are."

"Thanks again, Uncle Javier."

"You're welcome. See you soon."

Gabby hung up and turned to Sarah, who was watching her. "It's done! We're going to Miami!"

Saturday, February 21

Homicide Division
Flagler Street
9:15 a.m.

Eva came in to find Luis already at his desk. "Morning."

"Good morning, Eva. Get any sleep last night?"

"Not much. Does it show?"

Luis laughed. "No. You look nice, as always."

"Then how did you know?"

His smile disappeared. "I've been your partner long enough to know how a story like the one we heard yesterday impacts you. I'm guessing you couldn't get rid of the anger to go to sleep."

Eva dropped into her chair and held up her hand. "Guilty as charged."

Despite being the junior member of the team, Luis wasn't going to sit by and let her torture herself without putting in his two cents. "You've been a cop a long time, Eva.

You know, and I know, it'll eat you alive if you let it."

"I know, I know. Usually, I can push it out of my mind when I'm away from here, but it gets extra hard with someone like Estrada."

Luis stood. "I can sympathize. You want some coffee?"

"That'd be great."

While Luis was gone, Eva tried to organize her thoughts by talking to herself under her breath.

We need to make a stronger connection between Estrada and Bonita Mendez or we'll get nowhere with a request for a search warrant. Just because Estrada is capable of killing Bonita doesn't mean he did.

There was nothing at the crime scene from Estrada. There was nothing on Miss Mendez to connect her to him, either. So what do we have?

There's the phone call from Bonita Mendez to her parents, made from the same neighborhood as the Castle Hotel, and the suggestion from the dollar store owner that girls from the hotel come in there bruised. Add to that a suspicion, but no proof, that the Castle Hotel is a center for prostitution, and you have a bunch of what?

"A bunch of coincidences! We might as well connect Estrada and Mendez by saying they both lived in South Florida!"

Luis returned with two cups of coffee. "What was that?"

"Oh, I'm trying to connect Estrada to the Mendez girl."

"Any luck?"

"Just the phone call to her parents from the Castle Hotel neighborhood."

"That's not a connection, that's an oddity, or best an anomaly."

"And the dollar store guy's tip about the hotel."

"I wouldn't call that a connection, either."

Eva let out an exasperated sigh. "Luis! You're not helping."

He sipped his coffee, smiling at her. "I'm sorry. I'm just stating the obvious, aren't I?"

"Yes. What do you think? Are we on the wrong track?"

Luis rubbed his chin and pondered their position. Finally, he shrugged. "I can't say. My gut says we're looking at someone we should, but that may just be because we have no one else to run down right now."

"So, until we find another rabbit hole, we continue to chase this rabbit?"

Luis nodded. "Agreed."

"Okay, then. What next?"

He grinned at her. "I have no earthly idea."

****

It turned out "what next" was more of the same. The two detectives went through the Estrada files again, then went to lunch. After their lunch break, they looked over the paperwork once more. Unfortunately, the result was the same.

Next, they reviewed all the evidence from the crime scene and autopsy, searching for anything that might point them in a new direction, but that, too, was fruitless.

Eva rubbed her eyes and checked her watch. Three-fifteen. She was considering taking off early and picking up Maria when her phone rang. "Hernandez."

"Yes, this is Jerry Carson from Parole and Probation. I spoke to you yesterday."

"Yeah, sure. Hi, Jerry."

"I was thinking about our friend Javier Estrada and it occurred to me you might not be aware."

"Aware of what, Jerry?"

"He was the prime suspect in a homicide case up in Ft. Lauderdale that went cold several years ago."

Eva sat straight up in her chair. "Really? We didn't know anything about that."

"It occurred between Estrada's jail time for the assault and the attempted murder conviction, but he was never arrested."

"Do you remember the victim's name?"

"No, but the detective on the case was a friend of mine. Rick Garcia. He still works up there."

"Thanks for the heads up, Jerry."

"No problem. Tell Rick I said hi."

"Will do. Bye."

Luis was watching her. "What was that?"

She filled him in, then grabbed her phone. "I need to look up the number for Ft. Lauderdale PD."

Police Station
Ft. Lauderdale
Broward Boulevard
5:15 p.m.

Eva found Rick Garcia was more than glad to meet with her and Luis. The cold case of Brittany Walker had stuck in his craw for six years now. When Eva called, Garcia was on another case, but said if they wanted to come up right then, he would brief them. Eva and Luis had left immediately.

The drive north to Ft. Lauderdale took about an hour, and when they gave their names at the front desk, the officer pointed at the elevator. "Take it to the basement. Rick is waiting for you."

When they got to the basement and the elevator doors slid open, they found a man sitting by himself in a glass-walled room. A fit two hundred or so pounds and silver-haired with a moustache to match, Detective Rick Garcia vibrated with enthusiasm. He bounded from the table to meet the detectives.

"You must be Eva Hernandez, glad to meet you." They shook hands. "And you're Luis Moreno, right?"

Luis nodded as they also shook hands. Garcia turned back into the room. "Here, take a look at what I've got."

They followed him in and sat down at a large wooden table. Garcia sat opposite the detectives, the file spread out on the table between them. Eva immediately noticed the photos.

"Those are a match for our case. What did the medical examiner determine was the weapon?"

"Some sort of pipe was his best guess, but we never found it."

Luis took out a notepad. "You want to give us a complete rundown?"

Garcia nodded. "Sounds good. The victim was seventeen-year-old Brittany Walker. She was a runaway from Tampa and had been missing for a little over a year when she was found like this. Her body was discovered on a public beach near the Yankee Clipper."

Eva stopped him. "The Yankee Clipper?"

"Big hotel on the south end of the strip. Anyway, a couple walking on the beach found the body. It took us almost a month to ID her, but when we did, the family told us they had contact with her not long before her death."

Luis interrupted this time. "Was the missing persons still active?"

"Yes. The parents had filed it with Tampa PD and never rescinded it when she called. To them, she was still missing because she wouldn't tell them where she was staying." Garcia leaned back in his seat, the facts all coming from memory. "Anyway, when we went up to Tampa to do the death notification, they gave us a number from their phone bill. It was the number Brittany had called them from."

Rick leaned forward, picked a piece of paper up from the table, and handed it to Eva. "That's a copy of the phone bill. The highlighted number belonged to one Javier Estrada."

The similarities to their own case were eerie. Eva checked the area code. "Nine-five-four, that's Ft. Lauderdale local, right?"

Garcia nodded. "He had a house here at the time. It was during our investigation when he decided to move back to Little Havana."

She laid the paper down. "So, the million dollar question is—why did the case go cold?"

"Simple. We knew he did it, and he knew we knew he did it, but we had nothing more than a phone call to connect him." The big detective sighed. "Look, everyone was scared of the guy. Nobody we talked to would put Miss Walker with Estrada anywhere close to the time of the murder. Have you met Mr. Estrada?"

Eva nodded.

"Then you have a pretty good idea how the questioning sessions went. I've never met a cooler customer, nor a more arrogant one, and that has a lot to do with why this case bothers me so much."

"What about DNA or trace evidence?"

"There was semen extracted from her, but it was a mixed sample, and we could never get a match."

Luis looked up from his note-taking. "Did you ever tie Estrada to prostitution?"

Garcia shook his head. "The semen suggested it, but we could never prove that either. Again, no one would talk. He had a lot of people scared."

Eva picked up one of the photos. "I can see why."

Garcia nodded. "He's as bad as any I've ever seen. There's evil and then there's this guy."

The two Miami detectives exchanged looks and Luis closed his notepad. "Thanks for meeting us, Rick."

"Don't mention it. If there's anything you need, let me know."

"Can you send us copies of the autopsy and forensic reports?"

"Of course. I'll send them tonight."

Eva stood. "Thanks again."

On the drive back to Miami, Eva voiced her frustration. "That was as much help as I'd hoped it would be."

Luis shrugged. "I don't know. I think there's something there."

"What are you thinking?"

"Well, if you match the weapons and beatings, you begin to get a method of operation. His MO seems to be brutality with a pipe. If we can nail him for the Mendez girl, we might be able to get him for the cold case as well."

Eva smiled at her partner. "It's nice working with an optimist, you know that?"

"Why, thank you. That might be the best compliment you've given me yet." He laughed. "In fact, it might be the only one you've given me!"

"Oh, stop it! I've raved about your coffee-making skills many times."

He grinned at her. "Well, there is that."

Thursday, February 26

Apartment of
Sarah Potter
Fort Myers
7:45 a.m.

Six days had passed by in a flash. It had taken her less than three days to pack a few odds and ends along with her clothes, turn in the keys, and move over to Sarah's.

Sarah was equally busy; almost all her stuff was ready to go except for the handful of things she was still using. Until time to leave, Gabby was sleeping on the couch and the two were spending evenings planning their trip.

Yesterday, they'd given notice at work. Actually, it was less of a notice and more of an *'I quit.'* After their shift ended, they'd gone to the office door together and knocked.

"Come!"

Entering side by side, they stood in front of Attila's desk, smiling at him when he looked up in surprise. "What can I do for you two?"

In unison, they chirped. "We quit!"

The flustered manager stared at them. "Okay... Both of you?"

More unison. "Yes."

"And when is your last day?"

They produced their uniforms and laid them on his desk. "Let's just say we won't be needing these anymore."

Then, giggling like school girls, they'd walked out.

Sarah came out of the kitchen carrying two plates, each bearing a slice of pizza. She handed one to Gabby. "We need to call your uncle."

"Yeah. I'll do it now." Setting her plate on the coffee table, she dialed his number.

"Hola?"

"Uncle, it's Gabriela."

"Hi, Gabriela. How is the packing going?"

"We're almost done. We plan on leaving tomorrow."

"Oh, Bueno! Call me when you are close and I will give you directions to my house."

"Okay. See you tomorrow."

"I'm looking forward to it. Hasta mañana."

****

Javier closed his phone and turned to his manager. "They will be here tomorrow. Do you have the rooms ready?"

Rafael shook his head. "Not yet, but they will be by the time we need them. One is going in the Mendez girl's old room with Regina and the other in 205 with Laurie."

"Good. I think I'll take them out to dinner tomorrow night, let them spend a couple days visiting the city so their guard is down, then have a special meal for them at the house."

"You want me at your place for the dinner?"

"Yes. Leave Jose in charge at the hotel that evening and have Gary on duty as well."

"No problem."

Homicide Division
Flagler Street
8:15 a.m.

The Bonita Mendez murder case was beginning to go cold. Eva and Luis had spent days going over everything in the files. That included the crime scene photos, forensic reports, autopsy reports, interview notes from Bonita's file, the file from Ft. Lauderdale, and Javier Estrada's criminal record.

It was exhausting, frustrating, and at times, mind-numbing. Despite their efforts, nothing new had developed.

Eva beat her partner to the station this morning, and when she arrived there was a note on her desk.

Hernandez,

You and Moreno get with me in my office at ten.

Castillo

"Great!"

"What's great?"

Eva looked up to see Luis just coming in. “Here. Read for yourself.”

Luis took the note, read it, and gave it back. “I figured it was coming. She’s bound to want a progress report by now and is probably wondering why we haven’t given her one.”

Eva rolled her eyes. “Oh, she knows why we haven’t given her one. We’ve got nothing, that’s why.”

“I guess we should organize ourselves before then. Where do you want to start?”

“With Estrada. He’s our only suspect.”

“Suits me.”

Office of Lieutenant Roberta Castillo 9:50 a.m.

Eva tapped on the doorframe. “Lieutenant?”

Lieutenant Roberta Castillo looked up from the file she was studying. “Hernandez. Come in. Is your partner with you?”

“He’s on his way.”

“Good. Pull up a seat.”

Eva took the chair nearest the window and laid the file she was carrying in her lap. She liked the lieutenant, even though they hadn't ever socialized away from the office, but Castillo was a professional. She conducted herself the same way Eva strived for: confident, capable, and serious about her work.

Shorter than Eva, but with the same olive skin and dark hair, Castillo preferred to wear her uniform with her lieutenant bars displayed. She didn't adhere to the more relaxed code of detective dress in the Homicide division, and as a result, it left no room to question her authority. Eva found it unlikely anyone would challenge that authority, regardless of attire.

Luis came in a moment later, closing the door behind him. "Morning, Lieutenant."

"Good morning, Moreno." Castillo closed the file she'd been studying. "Okay, who wants to do the talking?"

Eva opened her folder. "I'm up first, Lieutenant."

Ten minutes later, the basics of the case had been laid out. Luis then took over and gave the lieutenant everything they'd learned about their prime suspect, Javier Estrada. When he was done, Castillo leaned back in her chair and closed her eyes. "Any idea where to go next with this one?"

Eva shrugged. “Not really. We need a new lead.”

“What about the media? Any new stories on the case run by them?”

“Not in the last couple days. I had a reporter ask me about the case, but she said what I gave her wasn’t enough to run another story.”

Castillo nodded. “The only thing she might be interested in would be an interview with Veronica Borrego, and we owe it to the girl to not let that happen.”

“Yeah. Besides, if we did that, she’d never help us again.”

The lieutenant studied her detectives as she replayed the facts in her mind, searching for something they had missed. “What about the two young people who found the body?”

“What about them?”

“Have you re-interviewed them?”

Luis shook his head. “Wasn’t sure if that would serve any purpose.”

“Well, here’s the deal. Without a new lead, I’m gonna assign the two of you to another case. So, I’ll give you another day to talk to the kids and see if that produces something. If not, we’ll have to set the case aside so I can put you back up for a new one.”

Eva stood. “Fair enough, Lieutenant.”

Luis also stood. "We'll check in tomorrow."

For the first time, Castillo smiled. "Good. Dismissed."

Apartment of
Sarah Potter
Fort Myers
2:30 p.m.

Sarah pushed once, then twice, and finally, with Gabby's help, the trunk latched shut on the Honda Civic. Sarah fell onto the trunk lid in exhaustion. "Got it! I didn't think it was going to close for a minute."

Gabby laughed. "Yeah, well, I don't want to be standing next to it when you pop the button and let it fly open."

"I know, right! Our stuff will probably go everywhere."

The small car sagged under the weight of the girls' luggage, most of which was clothing. Half of the tiny back seat was filled with boxes containing pots and pans, towels, sheets, and toiletries. A microwave and coffee pot took up the other half. All they had left to load were the basics they needed to get dressed in the morning.

They went back inside the apartment and collapsed on the couch. Sarah rented her apartment furnished as well, so at least they had something to sit on. Gabby sighed. "This moving stuff is a pain in the you-know-what!"

Sarah nodded. "You can say that again. But, it'll be worth it, don't you think?"

"I do. I'm really excited to get to Miami."

"Me, too. It's gonna be a blast."

Home of Patricia Givens Coral Gables 4:30 p.m.

Coral Gables was a bedroom community south of Miami, filled with rambling single-story homes on lush tree-lined streets. The cars in the driveways were mostly new, and backyard pools were more the rule than the exception. Patricia Givens' parents lived in just such a home.

The two detectives had secured a meeting with Tricia and her boyfriend, Bobby Tucker, for four-thirty, but Eva didn't have high hopes it would produce anything new. Still, it was better than shelving the case.

The late February sun was warm, a down-payment on more heat to come in the months ahead, and Eva found herself gravitating to the shade by the door. They rang the bell and before long, a pleasant-looking woman in her late forties answered. She looked comfortable in a t-shirt and yoga pants and her smile came easily. "You must be the detectives."

Eva produced her badge. "Yes, ma'am. I'm Detective Hernandez and this is Detective Moreno."

"Please, come in. The kids are on the back porch."

The detectives followed her through a modestly decorated home to a screened-in area out back. The two teens sat at a round patio table under a ceiling fan which rotated just enough to provide a comfortable breeze. Mrs. Givens gestured at two empty chairs. "Make yourself comfortable. Would you like something to drink?"

Both detectives shook their head, and Eva sat down. "We're fine." She placed herself directly across from Tricia and next to Bobby. “How have you two been?”

Tricia smiled. “Better than we were the first time we met you.”

Eva nodded. “No doubt. Thanks for taking time to talk with us.”

“We’re glad to, but I don’t know we can be any help.”

Luis opened his notepad. “Have you two gone over what happened that night?”

Bobby grunted. “Only about a million times.”

“Did anything come to mind that you hadn’t thought of before?”

Tricia shook her head. “Nothing. We walked to the guard stand, and Bobby was laying out the blanket when I heard a noise and looked up. I couldn’t tell where it came from but that’s when I saw the shape of someone near us.”

Eva held up her hand. “Wait! You heard a noise?”

“Yeah. I told you that.”

Luis flipped through his notebook back to the night of their original interview. He scanned it, then looked at his partner and shook his head.

Eva’s adrenaline surged. “Could you tell where the sound came from?”

“The parking lot, I think.”

“Could you see anything?”

"No, but it sounded like a car door. Actually, I take that back. It sounded more like a pickup truck door. You know, heavier."

"But you didn't actually see a truck?"

Tricia shook her head. "I was distracted by the person I thought was near us in the sand."

Eva inhaled a breath. "Okay, continue."

"Well, that was pretty much it, until Bobby came running back toward me."

Eva turned to the young man. "Did you hear the noise, too?"

"No."

"Is there anything else either have you may have forgotten?"

The kids both shook their head.

Eva stood. "Okay. Thanks again for meeting with us."

Mrs. Givens led the detectives back to the front door. Once in the car, they headed for the precinct. Luis re-read the notes from the crime scene again while Eva drove. "She never mentioned the noise. You think it's for real or imagined after the fact?"

"My guess is it was real, but she just didn't put two and two together the night it happened because of the shock."

"So, we want to find out what Estrada drives, is that it?"

Eva nodded, her face grim. “Yes, but even if it is a pickup, I don’t know if it will be enough to buy us more time on the case.”

Friday, February 27

Apartment of Sarah Potter
Fort Myers
9:45 a.m.

Despite being up early, it took longer than expected for the girls to pack the last few items, but finally they were locking the apartment behind them. Sarah removed the key from her key ring. "I just gotta drop this in the office and we're off!"

Ten minutes later, they were heading south on I-75, Latin music blaring on the radio. Half an hour after that, they turned east and started across the Everglades Expressway. They took turns choosing the radio stations and sang at the top of their lungs, ignoring the groaning coming from their overloaded little car.

An almost euphoric sense of freedom overwhelmed Gabby, the obligations and worries that came with taking care of her mother now in the past and a bright future in front of her. She looked over at Sarah, whose smile mirrored her own. "We're gonna have so much fun!"

Sarah laughed. "We already are!"

Homicide Division
Flagler Street
11:00 a.m.

Luis leaned around the edge of Eva's cubicle. "Lieutenant's here."

Eva stood, grabbed the DMV report identifying the cargo van owned by Estrada, and followed her partner to their boss's office. Roberta Castillo motioned them in before they could knock. Eva went to close the door but the lieutenant shook her head. "I've only got a minute."

Eva handed the report to her. "We spoke with the two kids who found our victim. Tricia Givens said she heard a sound that night, which they failed to mention during their first interview, and indicated she thought it was a pickup truck door closing."

Castillo looked at the report, then her detectives, raising an eyebrow. "Did she see it?"

"No. She was distracted by the figure of our victim in the sand."

"What made her think it was a pickup and not a car?"

"She described the sound as 'heavier' than a car door."

Castillo handed the sheet of paper back to Eva. "Heavier?"

Eva shrugged. "That's what she said."

"And so you think this van may be the 'pickup' she heard, is that it?"

Luis nodded. "Well, if you think about it, a van is better than the open bed of a pickup to transport a body."

The lieutenant leaned back in her chair. "What do you propose?"

"A search warrant, maybe?" Luis visibly cringed when he said it.

Castillo was incredulous. "For the van?"

Luis nodded, but Eva remained motionless. She'd told Luis it wasn't going to fly.

Castillo shook her head. "If you think I'm requesting a search warrant based on the description of a 'heavier' sound, without even seeing the vehicle, you're nuts!"

Luis grinned. "That's what Eva told me you'd say."

"Oh?"

"Well actually, I think her words were 'you're out of your mind,' but the point was the same."

Castillo looked at Eva, a smile coming to the lieutenant's face. "I figured you knew better."

Eva nodded. "It was a shot in the dark."

The lieutenant nodded. "I'll say. Okay, here's what's gonna happen. I know both of you have been working for nearly two weeks straight, so I'm ordering you to take the next two days off. Get away and get some rest. Then, when you come back, if nothing new has come in on the case, I'm putting you up on the case board. Comprendé?"

Both detectives nodded obediently.

"Good. Now make yourselves scarce!"

Sarah's Honda
Interstate 95
12:15 p.m.

Gabby took out her phone and called her uncle. It rang just once before he picked it up.

"Hello?"

"Hi, Uncle. It's Gabriela."

"Hey. Are you close?"

"Yes. We just passed Ft. Lauderdale."

"Oh, great. Do you have GPS on your phone?"

"I don't but hold on." Gabby covered her handset. "Do you have GPS on your phone, Sarah?"

"Yeah."

Gabby returned to her call. "Sarah has it on her phone."

"Good. Write down my address."

"Okay. Let me get a pen." When she had pen and paper, Gabby wrote it down. "I've got it."

"Put it in Sarah's phone and follow the directions. I'll be waiting for you."

"Okay. See you soon."

Gabby hung up and entered the address in the GPS app. Seconds later, they had directions and a time estimate. "We're only thirty minutes away."

Sarah grinned at her. "Awesome!"

Home of
Javier Estrada
Little Havana
12:45 p.m.

The girls turned down the short side street, passing a yellow caution sign bearing the warning *No Outlet* next to the green street sign bearing the name Palm Terrace. The dead end sign was re-enforced by tall fencing across the end of the road. The series of homes on each side were neat but small, all with fences around their yards.

"That's it there." Gabby pointed at the last house on the right.

A black wrought-iron fence surrounded the white stucco home, capped by a red clay tile roof. The grass was immaculately manicured, shaded by medium-height banana palms lining the front, sides, and back of the property. A white-metal security door was closed, but the wooden front door behind it sat open.

Sarah parked on the grassy swale outside the fence, and the girls sat staring at the house. Almost immediately, the metal door swung open and a man came out. He wore a broad smile across his tanned face, and his arms and legs were both dark beneath his Hawaiian shirt and Bermuda shorts. His hair was nearly shoulder length and more gray than black.

He moved quickly down the walk toward them, so Gabby got out of the car. "Uncle Javier?"

Coming through the gate, he held his arms wide. "Gabriela! I am so happy to see you." He embraced her in a big hug, then held her at arm's length. "You look so much like your mother!"

She smiled, but was lost for words. Javier looked across the car to where Sarah stood. "Who is this lovely thing you have brought with you?"

"Uncle, this is Sarah."

He waved at her. "Come, come. It is nice to meet you. Let's get in out of the sun and we can retrieve your things later, okay?"

Sarah came around the car and the three went into the house. Despite the lack of air conditioning, the house was markedly cooler than outside, with ceiling fans spinning in every room.

They entered into a small living room, decorated with only a few items. A TV, a couch, two recliners, and a coffee table made of driftwood and glass. Beyond the living room, they walked into a tiny kitchen, where glass sliding doors to a back patio allowed light inside.

He guided the girls back through the doors onto a screened porch which also had a ceiling fan. "Sit, sit. Would you like a beer?"

The two girls exchanged glances. Gabby nodded. "Yeah, that would be great."

"Okay. Make yourselves comfortable and I'll be right back."

When he had gone inside, Gabby scanned Sarah for a reaction. "What do you think?"

"He seems really nice."

Gabby smiled. "I told you! He was the same way on the phone."

Sarah looked around the yard, which ran back to an alley. "This place is great. It's really private."

"Yeah, not a big house though. I hope he has enough room for us."

Just then, Javier came outside with three open beers. "There's plenty of room. You two are going to share the master, and I am staying in the guest room."

Gabby was surprised. "Oh, Uncle. We didn't want to put you out of your room."

"Nonsense." He dismissed her concern with a wave. "What do I need a big room for? I'm happy to have you two share it."

"That's really nice of you."

After handing out the beers, he dropped down in one of the chairs. “Now, tell me about your trip.”

Two more beers later, they were done filling him in. He stood. “Are you hungry?”

The girls nodded.

“Then why don’t you go get your bags while I fix us some lunch? Your room is on the right side as you come in the front door.”

The master bedroom was not large, but it had more than enough room for the two twin beds. There was a six-drawer bureau for them to share and a shallow closet.

Gabby looked at her suitcases, then the closet. “It’s gonna be a tight fit.”

Sarah was unfazed. “It’ll be fine. It’s only temporary, right?”

“Right!”

“Getting settled?”

The girls turned to see Uncle Javier watching them. Gabby smiled. “Yes, and it’s great.”

“I’ve got some food ready.”

“Okay, we’ll be right out.”

He disappeared and Sarah headed for the door. “I’m starved. This can wait.”

Gabby laughed. “I’m with you.”

They found Javier seated out on the porch, fresh beers and sandwiches waiting for them on the table. Gabby recognized the sandwiches. “Oh Uncle, these are like the

Cubans mother made. Sarah, you are gonna love these!"

"What's on them?"

"Slices of ham, smoked pork, and Swiss cheese with mustard. They're yummy!"

Sarah tried a bite, then rolled her eyes. "Oh my gosh! That's fabulous."

Javier managed an awkward bow. "Thank you, but you haven't seen anything yet."

Gabby sipped her beer. "What do you mean?"

"I'm taking you two girls out for dinner tonight to celebrate."

"Oh Uncle, you don't have to do that."

He waved a finger at her. "I insist."

"Well okay, if you insist!"

Sarah laughed. "Yeah, if you insist, Mr. Estrada."

Javier smiled at Gabby's friend. "Why don't you call me Uncle Javier as well?"

"Okay. If you insist, Uncle Javier."

He laughed. "I most certainly do!"

Kinloch Park Middle School
Miami
3:30 p.m.

Maria Hernandez spotted her mother's car immediately and ran to climb in. "Hi, Momma. I didn't know you were going to pick me up today."

Eva accepted a kiss on the cheek. "I got off work early, so I came to get my favorite daughter."

"I'm your *only* daughter, Momma."

Eva grinned at her. "I stand by my statement."

Maria buckled herself in as Eva pulled away from the curb. "Momma, are you working tomorrow?"

"Why?"

"I was hoping we could go to *Carnaval*."

Carnaval-on-the-Mile, which took place in Coral Gables, was the kick-off for the Calle Ocho Festival in Little Havana. A celebration of Latin food, music, and art, the Carnaval took place in the days before the festival, and was the more family-friendly portion of the celebration. Eva usually had to work the event, but her orders to take a couple days off had come at just the right time.

She winked at her daughter. "You know something? I was kinda hoping we could go, too."

"Really?"

"Really! Do you want to go with me?"

Maria was vibrating with excitement. "Yes, yes, yes!"

"Okay then. It's a date."

OLA Restaurant
Miami Beach
8:00 p.m.

Since Uncle Javier only had a van, the three of them had taken Sarah's Honda Civic on their dinner date. Sarah had let Javier drive, and when he pulled onto James Avenue in the trendy Miami Beach area, the girls' eyes widened with awe. Rainbows of color reflected off the front of white stucco buildings and swaying green palms while people dressed in beautiful clothes strolled along the sidewalks.

The car stopped in front of a large set of concrete stairs that led up to a glass double door. A young man came and opened the car doors for Gabby and Sarah. Gabby was dressed in the only nice outfit she had, a knee-length yellow dress she'd saved for the occasional church service with Rosie. Sarah was in a long green gown she'd bought for a previous Christmas party.

Uncle Javier was in a suit, and after speaking with the parking attendant, stepped between the girls and took one on each arm. "Shall we?"

The girls nodded and they ascended the concrete steps to the maître d. "Welcome to Ola's. Do you have a reservation?"

Javier nodded. "The name is Estrada."

A finger glided down the page. "Ah, yes. For three. Please follow me."

They wound their way through white linen tables with sparkling silverware, set out beneath a low, warmly lit ceiling, until they came to an intimate table near the back. Sarah's chair was pulled for her, then Gabby's, while Javier seated himself.

"Your server is Theresa, and she will be right with you."

No sooner had the man left, a woman in her late twenties appeared, wine list and menus in hand. "Good evening. My name is Theresa and I will be taking care of you tonight." She handed a menu to each of them, then the wine list to Javier. “Can I get you something to drink?”

Javier returned the wine list. “Yes, I’d like a bottle of Salice Salentino.”

“A very nice red, sir. I’ll be right back.”

Javier studied his guests. “You both look wonderful. Do you like red wine?”

They nodded together. Gabby opened her menu, then peered over the top at Javier. “This is so expensive, Uncle.”

“Nothing is too good for my niece.”

“I wouldn’t know what to order.”

He smiled. “Would you like me to order for you?”

Gabby closed her menu. “That would be great.”

Sarah hadn’t even opened her menu yet. “That goes double for me.”

“Very well. You two sit back and enjoy your evening and I will do all the hard work of ordering!”

He said it with such flourish that the two girls giggled. The waitress returned with the bottle of wine, opened it, poured a sample for Javier, then waited while he tasted it.

He nodded approvingly. “Bueno!”

Theresa poured all of them full glasses then disappeared. When she returned a few minutes later, she carried a basket with rolls wrapped in white linen, which she set down, then paused by the table. "Are you ready to order?"

Javier smiled broadly. "I will be doing all the ordering for these lovely ladies and myself. Let us begin with chicharron, then we will have pollo criollo for the main course, and finish it with three chocolate cigars!"

Theresa nodded and disappeared. Gabby cast a cautious eye at her uncle. "Chocolate cigars?"

He laughed. "With candy matches!" He lifted his glass. "To new and profitable adventures, si?"

The girls clinked and chanted together. "Si!"

An hour and a half later, they were finishing their second bottle of wine with their chocolate cigars, which turned out to be some kind of rolled cake. Gabby was beyond happy. Javier dripped the last of the wine into his glass. "So, I have big plans for your day tomorrow."

Gabby drank the last of her wine. "More plans? What now?"

"Carnaval!"

Sarah slurred a bit. "A carnival?"

Javier smiled at her. "No, not *a* carnival; *Carnaval*!"

"What's that?"

"It's a celebration that takes place on the streets of Coral Gables. There's music, food, art, and dancing. You will love it."

Sarah giggled. "If you say so."

"I do! Let us go before I order more wine."

Gabby found her way to her feet. "I agree. I am full and, I think, a little drunk."

Ten minutes later, they were on their way home.

Saturday, February 28

Home of
Javier Estrada
Little Havana
10:45 a.m.

"Are you ready, girls?"

Gabby came out of the bedroom. "I am. Sarah is just about done getting dressed."

"Good. The earlier we get there, the less of a walk from where we have to park."

Sarah emerged from the bedroom. "I'm ready!"

They piled into the Civic and headed out. The day was already warm and the girls' spirits were high. Twenty minutes later, they had parked and climbed out to the rhythm of the distant street music. Each girl was in a t-shirt and jeans, but Javier was in his usual Hawaiian shirt and Bermuda shorts, this time topped with a white Panama hat.

Eventually, they reached the main drag. People milled up and down the street in a meandering stream of dancing, eating, singing, and visiting. It was vibrant and exciting. Gabby nudged Sarah. "Isn't this amazing?"

"It's awesome."

Home of Detective Eva Hernandez Little Havana 12:30 p.m.

"Come on, Momma! Let's go."

Eva adjusted her sombrero in the mirror. "Patience, Maria." Slipping on her sunglasses, she turned to daughter. "How do I look?"

"Amazing, as always. Now can we go?"

Eva turned to Isabella. "Are you sure you don't want to come with us, Mama?"

"I am sure. You two go and have a good time."

"Very well." Eva kissed her cheek. "See you around dinner time."

First to the car, Maria was already buckled in when Eva sat down. Her daughter looked festive in her turquoise sun dress and white leather sandals. It was clear her daughter had inherited Eva's flare for colorful clothes. "Ready?"

Maria rolled her eyes. "You know I am."

Eva laughed and started the car. Traffic slowed their progress, but thirty minutes later, they'd wound their way into Coral Gables and squeezed into a parking spot. Up and down both sides of the road, small canopies were set up, and under each was a vendor or sponsor with photos, food, or some other cultural information. Every so often, they would come upon a stage where different groups of performers would take turns playing their own version of salsa, rumba, or Latin jazz.

The air was filled with the aromas of Cuban food, mixing together to make an intoxicating blend of deliciousness. The street was packed with people moving from one end of the road to the other, most of them dancing more than actually walking.

Eva spent most of the time being dragged by the hand in her daughter's quest to see what was next. "Maria, slow down."

"I'm hungry. Can we eat?"

"Of course. What would you like?"

"Tamales."

"Okay. What flavor?"

"Chicken, please."

Eva secured a chicken for her daughter and a couple cheese for herself. They found a spot in the shade on the roadside curb and sat down to enjoy their treat. Eva found herself more relaxed than she'd been in weeks, even managing to ignore the persistent efforts of her mind to travel to her current case. She hoped Luis had been able to relax as well.

****

Javier stopped at a tent manned by an elderly gentlemen who was busy cranking juice out of a press. "Girls, would you like a glass of guarapo?"

They exchanged curious glances, then shrugged. "Sure."

"Tres, por favor."

The man grabbed three cups and filled them with juice from his pitcher. A lid, then a straw for each, and he passed them out. Javier paid the man, then turned to watch the girls try their first taste of the classic drink.

Gabby's eyes grew wide as the sugary liquid crossed her tongue. "Hmmm! That's good. What is it, Uncle?"

"Pressed juice from raw sugar cane with a squirt of lime."

"It's fantastic."

Javier smiled broadly, but was suddenly distracted by something across the way. Sitting in the shade and eating was a woman in a large sombrero. It took him a second to realize why she was familiar. *It's that detective.*

"Uncle Javier, there's some tables in the shade over there. Should we grab one?"

"No!" He glanced to his right. Further down the road, on their side of the street, was a bench. "Let's go grab that bench, instead."

"Okay."

They moved to the bench and the girls sat. Javier remained standing, his eyes fixed on the detective. Eventually, she stood and took the hand of a young girl, heading off in the other direction. Javier took a deep breath. "Ready?"

Gabby tossed her cup in the nearby trash can. "Sure. Where to now?"

"If we head this way, there's usually tents with Cuban craftsman making jewelry for sale. Let's go see if we can find you girls something pretty, okay?"

He led them off in the opposite direction of Detective Hernandez.

Home of Javier Estrada Little Havana 6:30 p.m.

Tired but happy, the girls and Javier arrived home just before dinner time, though none of them were hungry. All three sat out in the screened porch, each one nursing a cold beer. A short time later, Javier's phone rang. "Yeah?"

He nodded several times, then hung up without responding. He drained his beer and stood. "I've got to run over to the hotel. You'll find plenty of beer in the fridge."

Gabby started to get up. "We'll go with you."

"No. It won't take long and you two have already had a big day."

"But I was hoping to see the place we're gonna work at."

Javier shook his head emphatically. "Not tonight. You'll have plenty of time for work, soon enough."

Gabby shrugged and sat back down. "You're the boss."

He grinned at her. "And don't you forget it!"

Castle Hotel
Little Havana
7:15 p.m.

Javier came through the door to find Rafael talking with a client. He waited for the man to leave before speaking with his manager. "What room is she in?"

"203."

Estrada walked into the back room, grabbed the pipe, and headed up the stairs. Inside 203, he found a defiant Jessica lying on the bed, a pen in her hand. She'd locked her face in a stare of resolve, masking the true fear he knew his presence caused. He pointed the end of the eighteen-inch piece of pipe at her.

"What are you doin' with that pen? Maybe you're writing an apology to my client?"

"Not a chance! He was a pig!"

"You never refuse a client!"

He stepped closer, and Jessica recoiled. “He hurt me the last time.” Throwing the pen at him, she balled up near the headboard.

The pen hit him in the chest, fueling his rage. “You don’t choose the client—the client chooses you!”

Lunging at her, he rained blows down on her arms and legs as she attempted to protect her head. It was no use. His rage was uncontrolled, and when he finally stopped, she was motionless. There was blood everywhere. Estrada wiped the pipe clean on the bedspread. “Don’t ever refuse a client again!”

He left the room and returned to the office. Dropping the pipe on the desk in front of his manager, Javier stepped into the bathroom and changed his clothes. Coming back out, he threw his bloody clothes on the floor.

“Burn those, then get her and the room cleaned up. She won’t give you any more trouble.”

****

The girls were still lounging on the back porch when he returned a short time later. Gabby smiled up at him, noticing his change of clothes. "That didn't take long."

"Nope. Just a little housekeeping, that's all."

"Did you get dirty?"

He opened the beer he'd grabbed from the fridge. "No, why?"

"You changed your clothes."

Her uncle looked down at his outfit as if he hadn't noticed. "Oh, that's right, I forgot. I stained the other outfit while I was at the hotel." He joined them at the table and changed the subject. "So, what do you want to do tomorrow? Any ideas?"

Sarah shrugged. "I don't know. How about the beach, Gabby?"

Gabby raised her bottle and clinked it with Sarah's. "The beach! That sound's perfect."

Sunday, March 1

South Pointe Park
Miami Beach
10:00 a.m.

Sarah turned off MacArthur Causeway and headed south. Within minutes, they were parked in the South Pointe Beach parking lot and strolling toward the sand. Both girls wore bikinis and carried towels. Gabby had on a visor and Sarah a ball cap. The day had dawned warm and the ocean was calm, with only a slight breeze coming off the water.

They made themselves comfortable on their towels, and even though it was only March, they put on lots of sunscreen. They sat looking out at the water and watching the gulls wander the sand. Sarah sighed. “It’s beautiful here!”

Gabby smiled at her friend. “Aren’t you glad we moved?”

"Without a doubt. Your uncle is really nice."

Gabby nodded. "He said he had a barbecue planned for tonight, and he's asked his hotel manager to come over and meet us."

"That sounds awesome."

Gabby stood. "Let's go dip our toes in the water, what do you say?"

Sarah jumped up. "I say I'm gonna beat you there!"

The two girls raced for the shore, their laughter caught up on the breeze.

Home of Detective Eva Hernandez Little Havana 12:00 p.m.

Eva, her mother, and Maria arrived home from Sunday Mass, piling from the car into the house. Maria went to her room to change while Eva and Isabella fixed some lunch. They went out on the patio, enjoying the slight breeze and relaxing in the quiet.

Eva rarely got to unwind to this degree, and when her phone rang with

Luis's number on her caller ID, she groaned. Reluctantly, she answered. "Hello?"

"Hey, Eva. How's your day off going?"

"That depends. Are you about to ruin it?"

Luis laughed. "No, no. I just wondered what time you were going to head in tomorrow."

"I figured I would take Maria to school, so nine-ish, maybe?"

"Sounds good. See you then."

When Eva hung up, her daughter was watching her. "Do you have to leave?"

"Nope. How about a game of dominoes?"

"Good idea. Do you want to play, Grandmother?"

"Of course."

Maria took off to get the dominoes while Isabella made room on the table. Eva sipped her drink, thinking back to mass, and remembering the priest's words: "Be grateful for your gifts." She certainly was.

Home of
Javier Estrada
Little Havana
5:45 p.m.

Estrada was standing next to the grill when Gabby and Sarah arrived back from the beach. A smoky, citrusy deliciousness met them at the door. Gabby breathed deep. "What is that, Uncle Javier?"

"That is slow-cooked pork shoulder in mojo."

"It smells fantastic."

"It is and it will be done soon, so you two get cleaned up. Our guest will be here anytime."

Twenty minutes later, Gabby and Sarah emerged from the bedroom. They were just sitting down on the porch when a large man with a shaved head came through the front door. Javier went to meet him.

Rafael whispered as they came together. "We have a problem."

"Oh?"

"That Jessica chick died this morning."

Javier looked over his shoulder at the girls watching them, then turned back to his manager. "Put a smile on, you idiot! You will dump her this evening, yes?"

"I guess. Where? Haulover, again?"

"That will be fine. Now, let's meet the girls, and I told you to smile!"

Javier led the way to where the girls were sitting.

"Gabriela, Sarah. I want you to meet Rafael. He is my manager and will be your boss at the hotel."

Both girls stood and extended a hand, which the man shook, though without much conviction. "Nice to meet you."

They returned to their chairs as Javier produced a beer for his guest. "Rafael runs things for me so I can spend more time on the beach."

Rafael nodded, but didn't say anything. He just kept a smile plastered to his face. Javier lifted the lid on the grill. "Gabriela, could you get us some plates? I believe it's ready."

"Of course, Uncle."

Sarah stood with her. "I'll help."

****

The dinner was delicious, and Gabby stuffed herself on the pork shoulder, even trying some of the crispy skin. With the table cleared of plates, Javier and Rafael had gone into the kitchen to make something special for the girls.

Sarah nudged her. “That Rafael gives me the creeps.”

Gabby nodded. “I know. He’s the complete opposite of my uncle, just sitting there and saying nothing.”

“I’d want nothing to do with him if it wasn’t your uncle we were actually working for.”

“I feel the same way, but maybe it’s more a case of Rafael being nervous. We might get to know him and find out he’s really nice.”

“I hope so.”

The noise of the sliding glass door opening caused them to look up. Coming outside with two glasses was Rafael, followed closely by Javier, who had two more. “Here you go, ladies!”

Each of them was handed a glass with a brightly colored yellow liquid, a slice of lemon on the rim, and a straw. Gabby held hers at arm's length. "What is it, Uncle?"

"It's a Havana cocktail."

"What's in it?"

"Oh, well now, that's a secret. Try it."

Both girls sipped a small amount of the concoction. Sarah's eyes grew wide. "Yummy! That's delicious."

Gabby was nodding in agreement but still sipping. Javier took a small bow. "Thank you. Enjoy; there's more where that came from."

The men sat down and made small talk with the girls, but by the time half her drink was gone, Gabby was feeling sleepy. That's when she looked over at Sarah.

She laughed and pointed at her friend. "L…ook at Sarah. Sheee… is out cold."

Gabby became aware her words were slurring, but she didn't feel drunk. Instead, she was just very, very tired. Setting her glass on the table, she realized all conversation had stopped. Rafael and her uncle were sitting silently and staring at her. Then everything went black.

Monday, March 2

Kinloch Park Middle School
Miami
8:30 a.m.

Eva pulled into the drop-off area at Maria's school. "Have a good day, sweetie."

"I will, Momma."

Her daughter climbed out of the car as the phone rang. She gave a small wave to her daughter before answering. "Hernandez."

"Morning, Detective. This is Castillo."

"Oh, good morning, Lieutenant."

"I was going to put you and Moreno on the case board this afternoon, but plans have changed."

"Okay. What's up?"

"A body was found by a jogger this morning at Haulover. It's on the north end this time, but the age fits your current case, so I'm assigning it to you two. Can you reach Moreno?"

"Sure. You said the north end?"

"Yeah. In the nude beach area."

Eva smiled. "Oh, Moreno should love this! I'll call him now."

"Okay. Forensics is already on the way."

Eva hung up and called her partner.

"Hello?"

"Luis?"

"Morning, Eva."

"Good morning. I just got a call from Castillo. A body has turned up on North Haulover and she wants us to take it."

"How far north?"

"In your favorite spot. The nude beach."

Luis groaned. "Man, I hate that place. I feel so uncomfortable there."

Eva laughed. "You mean with all the nude people standing at the edge of the crime tape watching you?"

"That's exactly what I mean. It's just not my cup of tea."

"I get it. Meet you there?"

"Yeah. I'm probably twenty minutes away."

"Good."

Haulover Beach
North Miami
9:15 a.m.

Eva parked along Collins Avenue and got out of the car. Yellow crime tape flapped in the breeze across a path between the vegetation that led toward the beach. A uniformed officer kept people from ducking the tape. Eva approached, showed the officer her badge, and went around the blockade.

Twenty yards down the path was a group of people, most of which she recognized. Crime scene techs, coroner assistants, and a police photographer. As she walked up, Luis called to her from the far side of the group. "Eva!"

She nodded at a few of the crime scene techs as she made her way over to her partner. He was standing next to a female body, which was mostly covered by a large bush, with just one foot and one hand exposed. When she knelt down, she could see under the vegetation and get a better view of the dead girl. The similarities to their first Haulover Beach victim were obvious.

Luis was making a couple notes. "Injuries around the head and bruising to the body are consistent with the injuries to Bonita Mendez. In addition to that, she's naked, no ID and no personal belongings. Officers are searching the area."

Eva stood. "Who found her?"

"A jogger. I already talked to him. He comes through here every morning on his way to run on the beach. He spotted her foot."

Eva looked toward the far end of the path that led out onto the beach. Yellow tape was blocking that end as well. "What about drag marks?"

Luis shrugged. "None apparent, but that's probably because there was a lot of traffic along here before the jogger spotted the body. Apparently, a lot of people like to watch the sun come up in their birthday suits."

Eva laughed. "So the sand was too disturbed?"

"Yeah. There's no way to be sure which direction she was brought from, but there's insufficient blood for her to have been killed here."

"Yeah, and that matches Bonita Mendez as well. She was dumped, too."

The familiar form of Doc Fuentes came under the tape and walked toward them. “Morning, Eva. Hey, Luis. Are you two almost done?”

Eva nodded. “Yeah, Doc. You can extract her from the brush and look her over now.”

“Good. I’ll probably schedule the autopsy for this afternoon.”

“We’ll check in later, then.”

The detectives waited until the girl’s body was clear of the brush and they could get a better look at her. Luis made a note of the description as Doc Fuentes called it out.

White, twenty to twenty four, black hair, blue eyes. No tattoos, no distinguishing marks.

When he was done, he closed his pad. “Back to the precinct and the missing persons files, Eva?”

“Only thing we can do right now. See ya there.”

Homicide Division
Flagler Street
3:15 p.m.

Eva and Luis sat at their desks, frustration mounting, as description after description of missing women failed to match their victim. So, when Eva's phone rang, she was glad for the distraction. "Detective Hernandez."

"Eva, this is Ernesto Fuentes."

"Hi, Doc. Autopsy done?"

"Yes, and I've got something for you. Actually, two somethings."

"Great. We need the help."

"First, I've identified the victim through her fingerprints."

Eva waved at her partner, and Luis came to her desk. She wrote as Doc spoke.

"Jessica Dawson, age twenty-three. She was a runaway from Pittsburgh, Pennsylvania nearly six years ago."

Luis took the piece of paper and went back to his desk, putting the information into his computer. "Found her."

Eva nodded. "Okay, we've got her. What's the other thing you found?"

"This is something I've never seen before. Written in ink, up near the armpits, was a name."

Eva's adrenaline surged. "A name?"

"Actually, two names. One under each arm."

"What were they?"

"Left arm had *Estrada*, and the right arm had *Javi*."

Eva nearly choked. "You're serious?"

"Yes, why? Do they mean something to you?"

"They sure do."

"Well, I don't have the rest of the report done yet, but I'll fax you the photos I took of the writing."

"Great! Thanks, Doc."

She hung up and looked at Luis. "You'll never believe it!"

"Believe what?"

"Follow me."

They both got up and went to the fax machine. As the pictures came off, Eva handed them to her partner. Luis looked at them, holding them side by side. "You're right. I don't believe it. Can we get a search warrant with these?"

Eva headed for the lieutenant's office. "Let's find out!"

Home of
Javier Estrada
Little Havana
5:15 p.m.

Eva and Luis rode together. Two black-and-whites accompanied them. They pulled up at Estrada's home, one police car going down the alley behind the house while the other parked in front and went to the door with the detectives.

An officer stood on either side of the door, one of them using his nightstick to pound on the front door. There was no response. He did it again. "Police!"

The door swung open. Javier Estrada stood smiling widely at the detectives. "What is this all about?"

Eva stepped forward and handed him the warrant. "We have a warrant to search your premises."

"Based on what?"

"We have reason to believe you're connected to a murder victim we found today. We're here to search for evidence related to that homicide."

"What kind of connection?"

"Evidence found on the victim's body. Please step aside."

"Of course. I wouldn't want to interfere with a murder investigation, now would I?"

It only took thirty minutes to finish looking through the home. The modestly furnished home had no sign of illegal activity, in fact, it was *too* clean for the detectives' liking. Eva and Luis were standing in the front yard as the officers finished on the back porch.

Eva's frustration was obvious. "Nobody is that clean."

Luis didn't want to give up. "What about the hotel?"

"The warrant doesn't cover the hotel. We'd have to get another one, and after this, it'll likely be tougher to come by."

"But the dead girl didn't write on herself for nothing!"

"I agree, but the judge may not."

The radio in their car crackled. "Detective Hernandez?"

She went over and picked up the mic. "Hernandez here."

"Yeah, can I get you to come around to the alley behind the house?"

"Sure. What have you got?"

"There's a car parked by the back fence here. No plates and no documents, but it doesn't look abandoned."

"Be right there."

The two detectives walked through the house and yard to the back fence. Sitting there was a late-model Honda Civic. The officer stood staring into the open trunk.

Eva's adrenaline surged. "Got something?"

The officer shook his head. "Trunk is empty."

Relief washed over her and she turned to look at Estrada, who was watching them from the screened porch. “This belong to you, Estrada?”

“Nope. It’s just been sitting there.”

“How long?”

He shrugged. Eva turned to the officer. “Call for a wrecker. Let’s have it towed to impound. We’ll trace the Vehicle ID and have forensics look it over.”

The officer nodded and got on the radio. The detectives went to where Estrada was sitting. Eva stared down at the man, his smile still fixed in place. “We’re towing the car. Other than that, we’re done.”

“Good. Don’t let the door hit you on the way out.”

Eva resisted the urge to wipe the smile off his face. Instead, she promised herself she’d see the day his smugness was gone and the smile was on *her* face.

“We won’t.”

Tuesday, March 3

A Small Room
Little Havana
Early Morning

Gabby struggled to make sense of her surroundings. Her head pounded and the fog in her brain wouldn't clear. She tried to rub her head but couldn't get her hands to move. Slowly, things began to come into focus.

She was on a bed, her hands tied above her. Her clothes from the other night were gone, leaving her naked but not cold. In fact, the room was stuffy and hot.

Sarah!

She rolled her head to left and then the right. Sarah was on the bed next to her, also naked.

"Sarah?"

Her friend was motionless.

"Sarah! Wake up!"

A slight moan was followed by a fluttering of Sarah's eyelids. Then her eyes popped wide open. “Gabby! Gabby, where are you?”

“I’m right here next to you.”

Sarah’s head rolled in her direction. “Where are we? What happened?”

“I don’t know.”

Tears rolled down Sarah’s cheeks. “Why are we tied? Where are our clothes?”

Gabby was struggling with the same questions, filling her with fear like she’d never known. “Sarah! Sarah! You’ve got to pull it together and focus.”

After several moments, Sarah’s crying slowed. “Okay.”

“We need to call out. Maybe we can call attention to ourselves.”

“Okay. Help! Help, anybody!”

Gabby joined her. “HELP! Please help us!”

The door to the room burst open and standing in the doorway grinning at them was Rafael. “Call all you want! No one can hear you.”

Sarah resumed crying, but Gabby was angry. “Where are we? Where’s my uncle?”

“He’ll be here soon, and will explain everything to you in terms you’ll have no problem understanding.”

He came over and checked the ropes on both girls, then left the room, shutting the door behind him. The room fell into silence, except for the sobbing that came from her friend. Gabby's thoughts turned to her mother, and how Rosie had never mentioned her brother Javier, and it suddenly dawned on her why.

She was protecting me from him!

Homicide Division
Flagler Street
8:15 a.m.

Eva arrived to find Luis on the phone. He waved at her as she passed by on her way to the coffee machine. When she returned, he was just hanging up. "Morning."

He nodded. "Good morning. I just got off the phone with the Pittsburgh Police Department."

"Are they gonna go out to the parents?"

"Yeah. They'll notify them and then ask for any help. The detective I talked to said he would fax the interview notes."

"I bet he wasn't thrilled to get your call."

"No, and I don't blame him. Nobody likes doing death notifications."

Eva sat down with her coffee, nursing it with both hands. "What about the VIN on the Honda we towed. Anything?"

Luis opened his notepad. "Yes. The car is registered to a Sarah Potter of Fort Myers. It gives us an address but no phone number."

"So, I guess we take another trip across Alligator Alley?"

"Looks like it."

"Okay, I'll fill in the lieutenant and meet you downstairs."

"Good enough."

A Small Room
Little Havana
Mid-Morning

Gabby had been pulling at her ropes for what seemed like several hours, but she didn't actually know what time it was. The slim amount of light coming in through the lone window told her it was daytime, but that was all.

Her wrists were raw, but she was no closer to getting loose. Sarah had gone quiet, with only an occasional whimper. Gabby was fighting her own fear, as well as the guilt of having gotten her friend into whatever this situation was.

From outside the room came the sound of voices, followed by footsteps, then the door opening. Her uncle walked in. His ever-present smile from the last few days was gone, and his eyes were darker than any Gabby had ever seen before. She barely recognized him.

He flipped a light switch and she was temporarily blinded by the bulb overhead. "Uncle, why are you doing this?"

He ignored her, instead checking the ropes. Apparently unhappy, he barked for Rafael. "Get in here!"

Rafael appeared. "Yeah?"

"She's getting loose. Re-tie her."

Rafael obeyed while Gabby watched her uncle, now standing at the bottom of her bed. When the manager was done, he left the room again, shutting the door behind him.

Her uncle started to pace the small room. "So, ladies, this is how it's going to be. You now work for me, just like I promised. When I decide you're ready, you will have your first clients."

A chill ran down Gabby's spine. "Clients?"

"That's right. I have a group of men who pay good money for entertainment like you two."

"No, Uncle…"

Estrada moved toward her so quickly, she jerked. He leaned over the bed, staring down at her naked body. "Don't call me that! I was never your uncle, Rosie made sure of that. I never saw you once, in all the years."

"But how can you do this to your family?"

"You're not family. I don't have any family. You're just another lost girl who can make me some money. I'm your boss and I own you."

"I won't do it!"

He laughed. "Oh, you'll do it. They all do it."

"Well, I won't." Gabby spit at him.

His reaction was instantaneous. He drove his fist into her face, splitting her lip. "Don't be such a stupid girl. There's only one way for you to stay alive, and that's doing exactly what I tell you."

He moved over to Sarah's bed, and she tried to scoot away from him. "You'll be a good girl, won't you, Sarah?"

Her eyes were wide and her lip quivered. He ran his hand slowly from her chest down to her stomach, and she freaked, kicking wildly. Javier pounded her repeatedly with his fist until she lay quiet. He stood, looked down at Sarah, then at Gabby.

"You can make this hard or make it easy, but it will happen. I trust you'll make the smart choice."

He went to the door, flipped off the light, and left the room.

Gabby tasted the blood on her lip, and listened to the moans coming from her friend. The seriousness of their situation began to finally close in on her.

How can this be happening? Is it all my fault? Am I the stupid one to not have known?

Tears rolled down her cheeks and she became the one sobbing uncontrollably. Her body vibrated with fear and panic as she let go.

Apartment Building of Sarah Potter Fort Myers 1:15 p.m.

Twin Oaks Apartments in Fort Myers were a series of two-story buildings with first- and second-floor units. They located the number listed on the Honda registration and knocked. After a few minutes, they knocked again, but still with no answer. Luis walked around to the back where he could see through the patio door. "I don't think she lives here anymore."

"No furniture?"

"There's furniture, but it's all gathered in the middle of the room, like someone was cleaning."

"Okay. Let's check with management."

They found the office near the mailboxes in the center of the complex. Behind the desk, was a man in his mid-fifties, with salt and pepper hair. He wore a green polo with the Twin Oaks symbol, which appeared more like two palm trees to Eva. He looked up when they entered but didn't smile. "Can I help you?"

Eva showed her badge. “I’m Detective Hernandez with Miami PD. This is my partner, Detective Moreno. We’re trying to locate one of your residents.”

“What’s the name?”

“Sarah Potter. The address we have says she lives in apartment G-33.”

“Used to live in G-33. She moved out about a week ago, no notice or nothing.”

Eva exchanged looks with Luis. He pulled out his pad. “Did she drive a Honda Civic?”

The man went to a file cabinet and pulled a folder. “That’s what was listed as her tenant vehicle.”

“Did she say where she was going?”

He slammed the cabinet shut again. “No, and I wouldn’t have cared if she did. She came by, dropped off the key, and said goodbye.”

“What about her employer? Do you have that information on file?”

He returned to the cabinet, opened it again, and stared at the file. “Denny’s over on Marketplace Road. Anything else before I put this away again?”

“Did she leave a forwarding address?”

“Not with me.”

Luis closed his notepad and Eva produced a card. “Thanks for your help. Please call us if you hear from her.”

"Sure, but I don't expect I will."

Outside, Eva looked up the directions to the Denny's restaurant. "Fifteen minutes from here."

Luis nodded and climbed in the car. "Good. I'm hungry anyway."

Denny's Restaurant
Fort Myers
2:00 p.m.

The restaurant was in the lull between lunch and dinner, and the manager was more than happy to speak with them. He got the detectives coffee and sat at a booth with them. "Now, what can I do for you?"

Luis had his notes out. "We're looking for a girl by the name of Sarah Potter. We were told she works here."

"That's right. That is up until last weekend."

"Did she tell you where she was going?"

"Nope. She and Gabriela were taking off somewhere."

Eva set her cup down. "Gabriela?"

"Yeah. Sarah and Gabriela were friends who came in and quit together. Pissed me off!"

"What was Gabriela's last name?"

"Estrada."

Both detectives froze, staring at the manager. He looked from one to the other. "Did I say something wrong?"

Eva thought her ears were playing tricks on her. "Did you say Sarah's friend was Gabriela *Estrada*?"

"Yeah, why?"

"Do you have Miss Estrada's address?"

"In the office. You want it?"

"Yes, please. Did they ever mention going to Miami?"

The manager shrugged. "Not that I remember. I'll send Carol over while I get the address. She might know."

He waved at the waitress filling salt shakers a couple tables away. When she came over, the manager explained. "Carol, these detectives are looking for Sarah Potter."

The waitress sat down while the manager went to his office.

Carol was obviously worried for her two friends. "Are they okay?"

Eva struggled to focus with her mind going a thousand miles an hour. "We don't know. We just need to talk to her. Do you happen to have her cell number?"

"Yeah. It's in my phone." She pulled out a cell phone in a bright pink case and scrolled down a few times. "Here it is. 555-3692. Sarah said they were going to Miami to work for Gabby's uncle."

"What about Gabriela's phone number? Do you have it?"

"Sure. It's 555-2040."

Luis was scribbling as fast as he could. "Did they say where the job was?"

"Something to do with a hotel he owned, I think."

The manager returned with a slip of paper. "That's the address. Gabriela lived not far from here."

That was all the two detectives needed. They downed the rest of their coffee, thanked both Carol and the manager for their help, and bolted for the door.

An hour later, they'd determined Gabriela Estrada had left her apartment also, and with that, they were on their way back to Miami. As Luis drove, Eva got on the phone to Lieutenant Castillo, giving her both girls phone numbers. "We need the phone company to ping those for us on the off chance their cells are still active."

"I'll get it done. You want the phone records, too?"

"Please."

"Okay. See you when you get back."

A Small Room
Little Havana
Late Afternoon

"Gabby, are you awake?"

"Yes. Are you okay, Sarah?"

"I think I have a broken tooth and my head hurts. What are we gonna do?"

"I don't know, Sarah. I don't know."

"I think he wants to make us into prostitutes!"

Gabby realized Sarah was still not comprehending the entire situation. "It'll be okay."

"I can't do it, Gabby. I rather be dead."

"Listen to me, Sarah. We do what we have to in order to survive. That's all. I'll find us a way out of this, but in the meantime, we have to stay alive! You hear me?"

The only answer was more sobbing.

"Sarah?"

"What?"

"I'm sorry."

The room fell silent, no answer coming from Sarah. Gabby hadn't expected one.

Homicide Division
Flagler Street
10:45 p.m.

Eva sat at her desk going over the phone records from both girls. They verified the contact with Estrada, but didn't help locate where they were now. Both phones had pinged near Estrada's home, but neither had been active in nearly two days. The phone silence was ominous and chilled Eva.

Lieutenant Castillo tossed a folded sheet of paper on Eva's desk. "There's your warrant. Sorry it took so long, but I had to track down a judge. Take two black-and-whites with you."

"Does it include the van?"

"Yes, but it's based on the search for the missing girls, nothing else."

"I've already got a BOLO out for them. Luis is downstairs talking to the sergeant on duty and getting a team together.

We plan on using fresh officers from the midnight shift change to serve the warrant."

"Okay. What time did you plan on hitting the place?"

"By the time we're ready, I would say between two and three a.m."

"Good. Keep me advised."

"Yes, ma'am."

Luis came around the corner just as the lieutenant was walking away. "Did we get it?"

Castillo pointed back at Eva, and his partner waved the sheet of paper at him. "Right here."

"Okay. Sergeant Alvarez said we can have two teams that come on at midnight. We'll be able to brief them and go any time after that."

"Good. Let's go over the plan one more time."

Wednesday, March 4

A Small Room
Little Havana
12:15 a.m.

Weak from hunger, Gabby had dozed off, and now woke up to find Sarah gone. Panic filled her as she pulled at her restraints, calling her friend's name, but she was interrupted by yelling from the next room. It was Sarah.

"No, no! Please don't!"

"Shut up!" It was a voice Gabby didn't recognize.

Several loud thumps, like somebody being hit, came through the thin wall next to her. They were followed by sobbing from Sarah.

Tears flowed down Gabby's face as fear unlike any she'd ever known took control. Then the door opened, revealing a man she'd never seen before.

No, oh no!

Castle Hotel
Little Havana
2:15 a.m.

One of the police units went down the alley behind the hotel, another unit arrived from the south, and the two detectives came in from the north. It all happened within a few moments. Eva pushed through the front door, followed by Luis with warrant in hand.

Rafael was at the front desk. “What’s going on here?”

Luis handed him the paper. “This is a warrant to search the hotel premises. You will sit over there and not move.”

“I need to call the owner.”

Luis took the manager’s arm, bending it up behind him, and steered him to the chair. “Later.”

Eva instructed the two officers to secure the main commons area while she went through the back office. Luis started going through the check-in book at the front desk.

Ten minutes later, one of the officers returned. “Most of the rooms were unoccupied except for several on the second floor. Each claims to be a resident, not a guest. They're secured in their rooms. The unit in the alley reports no activity."

Eva nodded. "Thanks. Let's bring the residents down to the commons, but keep them separated."

"Yes, ma'am."

Eva searched the back office and found nothing. Just mundane records from a poorly run hotel. She returned to the front desk. "Anything?"

Luis was flipping pages on the hotel registry. "Just a lot of short-term guests."

"How short?"

"Hours, mostly."

She snorted. "Figures."

The officer returned. "They're ready."

Eva thanked him. "I need you to stay here with him. No phone calls."

"Yes, ma'am."

"Come on, Luis. Let's go see what the residents have to say."

The Castle Hotel had been constructed around a central courtyard with only windows to the outside exterior of the building, most of which were barred. All the doorways opened to the common area, which was exposed to the sky above.

They found six women seated at different locations around the commons, none older than about twenty-five. The officer watching over them showed Luis a list of names, most of which if not all, the detective figured would be fake. He instructed the officer to run them anyway for a records check.

Eva, holding a pair of photos, had started with the girl sitting nearest the office. "Do you recognize either of these women?"

The girl, blond and thin, shook her head.

Eva pressed. "You sure?"

"I'm sure."

"Is there anything I should know about your living here?"

"What do you mean?"

"Are you here voluntarily?"

The girl's gaze flipped to the office door, then back to the detective. "Of course. Why?"

"Just wondering. How's your relationship with the owner, Javier Estrada?"

"Is that his name? I hardly ever see him."

"Oh? What about the manager, Rafael? He ever give you any trouble?"

The girl's eyes dropped, avoiding Eva's stare. "No problems."

"Sure?"

"I'm sure. Can I go back to bed, please?"

"In a little while. Sit tight for now."

Eva moved on to the next girl with the same result, and then the next. Luis was working his way from the other end, and soon they were done.

The officer who had run the names of the girls returned to Luis. “None of the names show up in the system.”

“No surprise. We could get their real names with fingerprints, but that’s not our focus right now.”

Eva joined them. “Nobody claims to have seen the missing girls. Let’s go through every empty room next. Bring the officers from the alley in and have them help. Get the keys from the manager.”

The officer nodded and left.

“You get the runaround also?”

Luis nodded. “Nobody has seen a thing.”

“They’re scared.”

“That’s definitely the vibe I get.”

“How can you blame them? No doubt they’re all aware of what happened to Bonita and Jessica.”

“The missing girls must be held somewhere else.”

Eva’s face revealed her frustration. “Yeah, but we’ll wait for the search to be complete before we give up. We also need to get a BOLO put out for the van.”

****

Two hours later, the search was over and the officers were leaving. Luis and Eva were last out the door, but they showed the photos to Rafael first. “You know these women?”

Eva detected a flicker of recognition. “Never seen ‘em before.”

“I think you’re lying!”

“And I think you’re keeping me from getting my beauty sleep.”

She debated pushing harder, but there was no point. She needed something on him, then she could make the guy squirm.

“Fine. Have a nice night. See you soon.”

A Small Room
Little Havana
4:45 a.m.

Estrada’s phone rang as he sat at the bottom of Gabby’s bed. “Hello?”

“It’s me. We had visitors this morning.”

“Who?”

"The two detectives. They had a warrant to search for them two girls."

"What happened?"

"Nothing. The women all behaved themselves, and they didn't find the pipe."

"That's because I had it with me. Why didn't you call me before now?"

"They wouldn't let me."

"Alright. Get Jose to cover the hotel, pick up some food for these two, and get over here."

"There's something else."

"What?"

"Their warrant covered your van."

"Son of a… okay. Get a move on."

He hung up.

Those detectives are starting to get on my nerves.

Home of Javier Estrada Little Havana 6:15 a.m.

Javier had only been home twenty minutes when a black-and-white police car pulled up in front of his house. Two officers approached the door and knocked. He was waiting for them.

"Yes?"

"Javier Estrada?"

"Yes."

"We've been sent to bring you downtown for questioning."

"Am I under arrest?"

One officer shook his head. "No, sir. Not at this time, but detectives have some questions for you."

"What about?"

"I'm not privy to that information, I'm afraid."

Javier considered his options.

I can refuse, but I'll look like I'm hiding something. If I refuse, they can probably get a warrant to question me, which means being booked into the jail before the questioning.

"Very well. I'll meet you down at the station."

"I'm afraid our orders specifically call for us to transport you."

Javier hesitated, then relented. "Okay. Let me get my wallet."

A minute later, he returned to the front door, locked it, and walked out to the squad car with one officer in front and another following. He slid into the backseat, and they were on their way in minutes.

Homicide Division
Flagler Street
8:45 a.m.

Eva hadn't arrived home until nearly six in the morning, but she'd been able to grab a two-hour nap before returning to the station. Luis had done the same while Estrada was being picked up for questioning.

She was looking through the one-way glass at him when Luis came into the room, shaking his head. "I just talked to the officers who picked him up. They searched the front and back of the property but didn't find the van."

"He's probably hidden it. I'd bet that van is the key to locating the girls, and to solving our homicides. We *have* to find it. Let's see what our friend Mr. Estrada has to say."

They left the observation room and filed into the brightly lit interrogation space. Estrada smiled up at them. "Good morning, detectives. I was beginning to wonder if you were coming."

Eva sat down at the desk while Luis leaned against a side wall. She took out a portable tape recorder and set it on the table. "You don't mind if I record our little chat, do you?"

"Not at all."

"I guess you've learned about our visit to your hotel by now?"

"My manager called me. He said you woke all my residents up. Kind of inconsiderate, don't you think?"

"Well, the thing is, we're looking for a couple of young ladies who have been connected to you."

"Oh?"

"Yeah, and we're concerned for their well-being."

Luis produced the same two photos they'd shown the women at the hotel, laying them on the table. Eva pointed at them. "Recognize either of these two young ladies?"

Estrada glanced at the pictures without leaning forward, keeping his distance from the the photos. "Nope. Don't think I've ever seen them before." He leered at Eva. "They're cute though."

Eva refused to take the bait. "Well, what's interesting is, we have a witness that says these two girls were coming to Miami to see you."

"Me? They must be mistaken. Who would this witness be?"

Eva ignored the question. "Where's your van, Estrada?"

"My van?"

"Yeah. The panel van registered to you is missing and we have a warrant to search it."

"Oh, that van. It was stolen yesterday."

Eva raised an eyebrow. "Stolen? Did you report it?"

"Not yet. In fact, I was going to do it this morning, but as you know, I've been pre-occupied with other matters. Perhaps you could file the report for me now?"

Eva smiled, shaking her head. "Afraid not. You can take it up with the front desk when we're done here."

Estrada looked at Luis, then back at Eva. "Speaking of done... Do you think we could wrap this up? I've got a business to oversee."

The detectives exchanged silent nods. Eva stood, picked up her recorder, and went to the door. She stopped. "There's one other thing I need to check. We'll send the officers in to get you after I verify it."

Luis followed her out the door, and they went to the observation room. Luis gave her an inquisitive look. "One other thing to check?"

Eva nodded. "Yeah, but right now I forget what it was."

Luis laughed. “Let him sit for a while?”

“Yeah. Tell the officers who picked him up to wait thirty minutes, then offer to help him file the stolen van report. In the meantime, let’s get with the lieutenant. We need more resources to find those girls.”

A Small Room
Little Havana
1:45 p.m.

Gabby sat on the bed rubbing her wrists. She’d promised to behave herself and so now she could be in the room without being tied to the bed. The first thing she’d done was take up the sheet from the mattress and wrap herself in it.

She still hadn’t seen Sarah since the first day, but could hear her in the next room. Rafael had brought some food and she’d been given a bottle of water. He never stayed in the room, but left and locked the door each time.

When she’d asked to use the bathroom, he’d pointed at five-gallon bucket in the corner. “That’s your bathroom.”

"Can I see Sarah?"

He'd left without answering. Now, she got up and went to the window, pulling on it to try prying it open. It was nailed shut and covered by a piece of wood on the outside. A noise at the door sent her scampering back to the bed.

Rafael swung it open and allowed a man inside, then shut the door behind him. The lock snapped again and the man came toward her. Gabby clutched at the sheet around her but it was no use. She lay back and closed her eyes.

Through the wall, she heard Sarah putting up a fight, only to be beaten into submission. Gabby tried to drown out what was happening with a chant.

Stay alive, Gabby. Stay alive, Sarah. Stay alive, Gabby. Stay alive, Sarah. Just stay alive!

Office of Lieutenant Roberta Castillo 4:30 p.m.

Roberta Castillo studied her two detectives as they entered her office and sat down. To say they were dragging was an understatement. Luis shut the door behind them and collapsed into a chair next to Eva. The lieutenant admired the detectives in her squad who put their cases before their own needs, and she understood, because she had been one of those detectives not so long ago. "Bring me up to speed."

Eva started, recounting the search, the interviews, the interrogation of Estrada, and his stolen van story. When she was done, Luis took over. "We've got a BOLO out on the girls and the van, but nothing so far."

"Okay. What next?"

"We need a warrant."

Castillo pulled a pad toward her. "For what?"

Luis tore a piece of paper from his own notepad and handed it to her. "These phone numbers."

"What are they?"

"The Castle Hotel and Estrada's cell phone."

"I'll get started on it immediately. Any other ideas?"

Eva nodded. "We'd like to get the photos of the girls and the van out to the media."

The lieutenant looked at her watch. "It's too late for the evening news. How about a news conference in the morning?"

Both detectives nodded.

"Okay. I'll arrange it. You two go home and get some shut-eye. The conference will be set up for nine in the morning and I don't want to see either of you until eight-thirty." Neither detective had the energy to argue with her. "Alright then, beat it."

They were gone in less than a minute, leaving the lieutenant to make a call.

"Public Relations."

"Amanda?"

"Yes."

"This is Roberta Castillo."

"Hey, Roberta. What can I do for you?"

"I need a press conference tomorrow morning, nine a.m."

"Okay. Usual media outlets?"

"Yes."

"What's the purpose?"

"Two missing girls."

Amanda whistled. "Wow. That oughta get them here. Consider it done."

"Thanks. I appreciate it."

Castillo hung up.

Now the warrant.

Thursday, March 5

Media & Conference Room
Homicide Division
Flagler Street
9:00 a.m.

The large room the police used for press conferences and meetings was state of the art. A huge projection screen ran across the front wall, above a raised stage complete with a polished wood podium in the center. The other walls were light-grained wood, and rows of black, padded chairs stretched from near the stage toward the back of the auditorium.

When Castillo, Eva, and Luis entered, they found the room over half full, and several banks of cameras set up near the back. Amanda from Miami PD public relations was testing the microphone. "Check, check."

Lieutenant Castillo nodded at Amanda before stepping up to the podium. Amanda signaled toward the back and the video screen lit up. Eva and Luis stood next to the PR director. Castillo turned to look at the pictures, then back at the press.

"Good morning and thank you for coming. The pictures you're looking at are of two women we are attempting to locate. The one on the left is eighteen-year-old Gabriela Estrada. The last confirmed sighting of her was in Fort Myers. The picture on the right is Sarah Potter. She is nineteen and was also last seen in Fort Myers."

Castillo nodded at Amanda again, who changed the picture. A photo of a van came up next. "This is a picture of a van similar to the one we're looking for in connection to the missing girls. We have copies of all three pictures, along with more complete descriptions, and the van's license plate number, in a handout that will be available at the door."

She stopped, and Amanda had all three pictures put up together. Castillo looked out over the room. "Questions?"

A female reporter in the second row raised her hand. "Are the girls considered to be in immediate danger?"

"We *are* concerned for their safety. We do not *know* if they are in harm's way, but we are definitely interested in making sure they're okay."

"How long have they been missing?"

"It's been six days since we have had a confirmed sighting of them."

A male reporter near the back stood. "Do you have a hotline set up?"

"Anybody with information can call the precinct or Crimestoppers."

"Is there a reward?"

"Not at this time."

A Miami Herald writer who Castillo was familiar with was leaning against the wall on the far side. "Lieutenant, why are they suspected of being in Miami?"

"The last information we have on their planned destination was Miami. We believe they were moving to this area and we have some confirmed activity on their cell phones in this area."

After a few minutes, no further questions came, so the lieutenant ended the press conference. "Thank you for coming, and please get a handout before you leave."

The two detectives followed their boss out to the elevator. Eva spoke for all of them. "Here's hoping for a change of luck!"

When they arrived back at their desks, the subpoenaed phone records were waiting for them. It was not a small pile, but the detectives were glad to see them. Even the monotony of searching pages of phone numbers beat sitting around waiting for the phone to ring with a tip.

Luis grabbed his coffee cup. “You want a cup?”

Eva nodded and handed hers to him. “Thanks. I’ll split the pile and we can get started.”

“Fair enough.”

When he returned, she had already begun.

Three hours later, they had each made multiple coffee runs, and hunger was starting to take over. Eva stretched her arms toward the ceiling. “I’m starved. You want to get some lunch?”

Luis leaned back in his chair. “Sounds good.”

“Have you found anything?”

“Nothing to get excited about.”

Eva pulled a pad on her desk closer to her. “Well, I’ve been checking the towers used for most of Estrada’s calls. Ninety percent of his cell traffic bounces off the same three towers. One near his home, one near the hotel, and one about midway between the two, which would be when he’s commuting.”

“Makes sense.”

“I’ve made special note of the towers that don’t fit into the pattern. There’s just a handful, so perhaps you can check them against the ones on your sheets?"

"After lunch?"

Eva smiled. "After lunch."

"Perfect. Let's go eat."

A Small Room
Little Havana
12:30 p.m.

Gabby jumped when the door opened, but it was Rafael with a bag of food and a drink. She had figured out that neither her uncle nor her captor took part in the dirty business of rape; they reserved that for clients, so her immediate fear subsided.

He handed her the burger bag and drink. Her thirst was overwhelming and she guzzled most of the drink before even opening the food sack. Inside was a small burger and fries, barely enough to curb her hunger, but she dug in anyway.

Wrapped again in the only thing she had to cover herself, the same dirty sheet, she was partway through the burger when it dawned on her that Rafael hadn't left the room. He was sitting in a plastic patio chair watching her eat.

She'd watched crime shows on TV where the victim talked their way out of a situation. She ventured a try. "Thanks for the food."

He nodded but didn't respond.

She sipped her drink, which wasn't the usual soda from her previous meals. "What is this?"

"Gatorade."

"It tastes fu… unny."

Did I just slur?

She stared at the cup, suddenly aware her vision was blurring.

Oh, no. NO!

****

Sarah lay in her bed, the sheet pulled up to her chin, shivering. It wasn't cold in the room but fear had a constant grip on her. She hadn't seen Gabby in days, how many she wasn't sure, but every now and then she heard muffled conversation. That was the case now, but she couldn't make out the words.

She strained for a sign of what might be going on next door, knowing the same thing probably was going to happen to her. A thud came through the wall.

What was that? Did something hit the floor?

It was followed by a moment of silence, then a different noise.

What is that? Is that dragging?

Silence again, then her door opened. Rafael came in, flipped the light on, and handed her a drink and a food bag. "You've only got a few minutes before I leave."

Famished despite being bruised and bloody, she dug in, washing down the half the burger with the drink in less than a minute. She never got to finish the other half of her meal.

Homicide Division
Flagler Street
1:45 p.m.

Back from lunch, Eva and Luis moved into the Homicide meeting room. Eva had notes from searching Estrada's phone records and brought her pad, while Luis brought his half of Estrada's cell phone records. On one end of the room was a large laminated wall map of Miami. Eva grabbed a dry erase marker and started talking while she wrote. "Okay, the tower closest to Estrada's home is the one on West Flagler, here."

She made an X.

"The second tower that shows up regularly is the river tower, on the south bank of the Miami River, here."

Another X.

"The third tower is a block and a half from the Marlins Ballpark, here."

A third X.

"These three are easily explained by the normal routes he would take every day. What I found interesting was all the calls bouncing off this tower here. It's situated near the Sheraton Hotel at the airport." She made a fourth X, then put down the marker. "So what is over there that brings him near the airport?"

Luis started going down his own sheets looking for that particular tower. Within five minutes, he had multiple calls highlighted. "The same tower pops on my records, too. You think he's got the girls hidden near there?"

She nodded. "Makes sense, doesn't it?"

"It does. What's the range of a tower?"

"There's a load of factors to consider, but the last time I looked into it, the urban towers we have in the city are pretty limited. They're not meant to cover more than a couple miles because of the signal density."

Now Luis got up and went to the map. Taking the marker, he drew a circle around the fourth tower representing roughly two miles out. "If the information is semi-accurate, then we're looking for a needle in that haystack."

Eva studied the circle. It was no small area, but there was a silver lining.

"Huge sections of the circle are taken up by Miami International Airport on the west and Melreese Golf Course on the south. There's Palmer Lake on the north side and the Miami-Dade Transit's main bus facility to the south. That leaves two areas: one to the east and one to the southeast."

One of the two was Eva's own neighborhood and a chill ran down her spine at the idea of Estrada keeping those girls near her daughter. "We need to refine the BOLOs, and then get with the lieutenant."

Luis nodded his agreement and headed for the door, followed by Eva. They found Castillo just coming back from lunch. Luis waved the phone records at her. "Lieutenant!"

Castillo stopped outside her office door. "What have you got?"

"We think we narrowed down where the girls might be."

"Okay. Explain."

"Got a minute to look at something?"

Castillo nodded. "Where?"

"Follow me." He led her back toward the direction Eva was coming from. Eva turned and headed back inside the conference room, followed closely by Luis and the lieutenant. Once inside, Luis pointed at the map. "Show her, Eva."

Eva traced the circle with her finger. "Because of the airport, golf course and the lake, we've narrowed it to these two neighborhoods."

Castillo studied the map. "How did you come up with this?"

"Cell phone tower traffic. This area is an anomaly on Estrada's phone records."

"Okay. I'll get black-and-whites searching the area for the van. You brief the duty sergeant for tonight's shift."

Eva nodded. "Will do. After that, Luis and I are going out to help with the search."

"Good. Keep me up to date."

Search Area
Little Havana
9:30 p.m.

Luis turned onto North River Drive for the fourth time in the last five hours. With Eva tracing their route on a paper map, they had been driving block by block, only breaking for dinner. At least two black-and-whites were helping in the search, but so far nothing.

Every parking lot, every side street, every alley, and every business warehouse area had to be rolled through slowly and meticulously, checking for the missing van. Now that it was dark, car-mounted searchlights were being employed, and that made the going even slower.

Eva was about to call it a night when her radio crackled. “Detective Hernandez?”

She keyed the mic. “Go for Hernandez.”

“This is dispatch. I have a call from a patrol officer on Twenty-sixth Street.”

“Patch him through.” A couple clicks were followed by a hum. “This is Detective Hernandez.”

"Yes, ma'am. This is Officer Daniels. I believe I've found your van."

Eva adrenaline surged. "Where?"

"It's in the backyard of a house directly behind USA Recycling. Do you know where that is?"

Eva looked at Luis, who nodded and turned the car around. "Affirmative, Officer. We're on route now. Please maintain your position."

"Yes, ma'am."

Less than three minutes later, they pulled up next to Officer Daniels's car. His searchlight was focused on a van, barely visible from the street. Eva walked up to the officer's window. "How did you see it?"

"I was driving through the recycling plant's parking lot and spotted it over the fence."

"Have you verified the plate number yet?"

"No, ma'am."

"Okay, we'll do that. Can you get another car to take up position in the plant's parking lot?"

"Yes."

"Good. Thank you."

Eva and Luis approached the front of the small house. It was dark, not even a porch light, and the officers had to use their flashlights to get to the front door. Luis pounded. "Hello? Miami PD. Anyone home?"

They waited a minute or so, then repeated the banging. "Miami Police! Anyone home?"

When no answer came, they moved around to the side of the house where they could get a better look at the van. Eva shined her light on the van's plate number. They exchanged looks. "That's it."

Luis nodded. "It gives us probable cause to enter the house."

"Yeah. Let's get backup before we go in."

Within ten minutes, two more squad cars were on site, along with a tow truck. A door-ram was used to batter the front entrance, and they went in with guns drawn. The first officer called out. "Living room clear!"

Another voice. "Kitchen clear!"

The first officer. "Bathroom clear!"

Luis. "Back door clear!"

Eva opened the first bedroom door. A mattress was on the floor with a sheet covering it. She hit the light. "First bedroom clear!"

Luis showed up and entered the second bedroom. "Second bedroom clear!"

Eva put away her gun. "Dang it!"

Luis was already on the radio. "Dispatch, I need a record search of this address for ownership."

"Copy that."

While they waited, the two detectives went out back to the van. It wasn't locked, but when they opened the doors, it was clear they weren't going to find anything that wasn't microscopic in nature. The van had obviously been scrubbed and even smelled of Pine-Sol.

Eva gave orders for it to be towed to impound, then she and her partner returned to the bedrooms. With all the lights on, the second bedroom in particular revealed blood on three walls, as well as the sheet on the bed. Her heart sunk and Luis read her mind. "Betting it's the girls' blood?"

Eva nodded. "There's less in the other room, but it's blood just the same."

Luis received a radio call. "Detective Moreno?"

"Go for Moreno."

"The home is registered to Castle Properties, LLC. The corporate address is on Palm Terrace."

His gaze met Eva's as they both recognized the street name. "Copy that. Thank you."

They'd found the hideaway, but too late. Eva left for the car, slamming the house door behind her in frustration.

Now where? I can't get another warrant for the hotel without cause and he's not dumb enough to take them to his house.

She dropped into the passenger seat to wait for Luis. She pushed her brain to come up with something, anything to find the girls.

Castle Properties! Public records will have all the places registered to the LLC.

When Luis climbed in, she told him her idea. "Perfect. They don't open until morning, so you want me to drop you home? It's not far."

"Please. Forensics will be here for hours and they don't need us in the way."

"Agreed."

Friday, March 6

Castle Hotel
Little Havana
7:00 a.m.

The fogginess began to clear, replaced by the now-familiar headache from being drugged. Gabby tried to force her brain to process what little information was getting through, but it was several minutes before it registered. She was somewhere different. And she wasn't alone.

"Sarah?"

"Afraid not. Whoever Sarah is, she's not in here."

Gabby pushed herself to a sitting position. "Where am I?"

"Room 203 of the infamous Castle Hotel."

Gabby's vision cleared and she took in her surroundings. There wasn't much to see. It was a basic hotel room with two beds, a bedside table between them, a dresser, and a TV.

"The hotel?"

"That's right. Not exactly the Fontainebleau is it?"

The girl sitting on the other bed was thin with curly black hair, green eyes, and dark skin. When she smiled, it exposed a missing front tooth.

"Who are you?"

"Regina, and I'm your new roommate, or rather you're mine."

"Where's Sarah?"

"I can't be sure, but my guess would be in another room."

Gabby rubbed her eyes, then tugged at her hair, trying to get it out of her face. "Why are we here?"

"You don't know? You're here to work."

Gabby's brain had cleared enough to put things together. She and Sarah had been moved to the hotel to begin working for her uncle. Fear returned in full force as she realized she was still naked.

She pulled the sheet up around her and got out of bed, going to the door. Regina shook her head. "Don't bother."

Gabby tried the doorknob anyway. It was locked from the outside. "There must be some way to get out of here."

"Oh, there is. As a dead body rolled up in a bloody sheet."

Gabby shivered involuntarily. "They can't keep us locked in here all the time."

"No, and they don't. Eventually, you'll have your own room and when clients start showing up, they'll unlock your door. You can even go outside the room for a smoke."

"I don't smoke."

Regina laughed. "Whatever. You can get a breath of fresh air, but the hotel is built in a way that no one knows you're in here. Except the animals that pay for you."

"Why are we together now?"

"I'm supposed be showing you the ropes, so to speak. In reality, I'm the one who convinces you to go along with the program or else."

Gabby came back to the bed. "Have you ever tried to escape?"

"Of course." She pointed to the missing tooth. "That's how I got this gap in my smile."

"How many girls are here?"

Regina shrugged. "I don't know for sure. I'd guess between six and ten, most of the time."

Gabby realized she needed to pee. She went into the tiny bathroom, nearly vomiting from the smell. The shower head was screwed into some kind of a shut-off which had a padlock on it. She stuck her head out the door.

"What's with the shower head?"

"Oh, that. Showers are one of the rewards for meeting your quota."

Gabby's head started to spin and she thought she might pass out. She clutched the doorframe. "Quota?"

"Six hundred dollars a day. That's what he expects or no shower. Go too long without meeting quota and you get the pipe."

"The pipe?"

"It's an eighteen-inch piece of hell wrapped with duct tape."

Gabby staggered slightly, and dropped onto the toilet.

There's got to be a way out of here! I have to find it, if not for me, for Sarah.

Miami Government Center
Downtown Miami
8:15 a.m.

Luis picked Eva up and the two detectives headed directly for Government Center. A tall, beige building with modern, blue-tinted windows and a large courtyard, it represented the renewing of Miami's downtown. Every twenty feet, a tree had been planted in a space between the concrete slabs, giving shade for anyone wanting to sit.

Inside the Property Appraiser's office, they found a clerk willing to help. Eva stepped up to the desk and showed her badge. "We're looking for all properties under the ownership of Castle Properties, LLC."

"Did you use our online search tool?"

Eva had tried it at home the night before but couldn't search by a corporate name. "Yes, but it wouldn't give me what I needed."

The young clerk, who must have assumed that Eva didn't know how to use the computer properly, pulled out her keyboard. "Let me try. You said Castle Properties, LLC?"

Eva nodded, then looked at Luis, who rolled his eyes.

After a few seconds, the girl looked up. "Hmmm, nothing." She stood. "I'll be right back."

She disappeared into a back office area, then returned a few minutes later. "Apparently we can't search LLCs online. We'll have to do a manual search, and we won't have it finished until this afternoon."

Eva handed her a card. “Please call me when it’s done.”

“Of course.”

“Thank you.”

Room 203
Castle Hotel
9:15 a.m.

Gabby had finished in the bathroom, splashed some water on her face and came out to find Regina staring at the TV. They’d sat in silence for nearly two hours watching game shows on the screen, when the room door opened.

Rafael came in, threw a bag of food and a bottle of water on each girl’s bed, then went into the bathroom. He came out holding the lock from the showerhead. “Both of you take a shower after you eat.”

He went to the dresser and pulled out some clothes, throwing a shirt and shorts onto Gabby’s bed. “Put those on after your shower.”

Then he was gone.

Regina was already eating her burger but Gabby wasn’t hungry. Washing off the filth suffocating her was more important, and she went directly into the bathroom. Turning the water on, she let it get warm and stepped in. The cleansing may have been superficial, but it helped her feel human again. She washed her hair with the small shampoo available, then her body with a cheap bar of soap. Before she was fully rinsed, the water cooled, then went cold.

Fighting the urge to scream, she forced herself to stand under the freezing water until she was rinsed. Toweling off, she came out into the room. "I ran out of hot water!"

Regina sipped her drink. "Oh, yeah. I forgot to tell you. There's limited hot water, and I'll even have to wait for it to build up again. Your showers need to be fast if you don't want to finish in the cold."

Gabby picked up the shorts laid out for her and pulled them on. She could barely zip them up. "These are too small."

Regina shook her head. "No they're not. That's how they want them; tight."

Gabby threw the shirt over her head and pulled it down. It was a brightly colored half-shirt that barely covered her breasts and left her stomach exposed. Still, it was better than the sheet. Despite her reservations, hunger took over and she attacked her food.

At least my bottle of water is sealed.

Homicide Division
Flagler Street
10:30 a.m.

Eva rapped on the doorframe to Roberta Castillo's office. "Lieutenant?"

Castillo looked up from a file she was studying. "Yes?"

"Got a minute?"

"Of course."

Eva turned and waved at Luis, who headed toward her. The two detectives grabbed a seat, Luis having shut the door behind them. Eva took out her notepad. "We wanted to bring you up to date on last night."

"Good. Shoot."

"We located the van behind a house east of the airport. The house belonged to Castle Properties, which is registered to the home address of Javier Estrada."

"No sign of the girls?"

"They weren't there, but there was blood and we're waiting on the forensic report. My guess is they *were* there, but we missed them."

"Crap. What about the van?"

"It was spotless, at least to the naked eye, but it's at impound and will be gone over by forensics this morning."

"What's next then?"

"We went to the Government Center this morning to have a search done on Castle Properties, but it'll be this afternoon before we get it, as well."

Castillo's face reflected the same frustration her detectives felt. "Is there anything we can do now?"

Luis vented. "We can take Estrada in for questioning again, but we're not sure it would get us anywhere. Can we ask for another search warrant on the hotel?"

Castillo shook her head. "Not without new evidence to prompt one. Any other ideas?"

"We were thinking about setting up surveillance."

"Okay. On?"

"The Castle Hotel. We think it has to be the key, unless we can find another property he's using to hide them."

"So you think he's moved them to the hotel?"

Both detectives nodded.

The lieutenant shrugged. "I'm sorry, but I don't have the available resources right now."

Eva closed her notepad. “We’d like permission to do it ourselves. Six on and six off.”

Castillo raised an eyebrow. “Starting when?”

“Tonight.”

The lieutenant’s gaze moved from one detective to the other. “Fine, I’ll keep you off the case board for three days. But you sleep tonight and start tomorrow morning.”

Both detectives stood. “Thanks, Lieutenant.”

“Good luck.”

Room 203
Castle Hotel
11:15 a.m.

Gabby was startled by a cell phone buzzing. Regina reached into the nightstand drawer and grabbed it. “Yeah?”

She listened, nodded, and closed the phone. “I’ve got a client. You can go outside the door for a while.”

Gabby stared at her roommate but didn’t move. A knock came at the door.

Regina turned off the TV. “Let him in on your way out.”

Gabby still didn’t move. Regina stared at her. “Unless you want to watch, you better get moving.”

Finally, Gabby got up, and opened the door. A short man in his mid-fifties stood back to let her pass, looking her up and down as she did. Then he disappeared into the room, closing the door behind him.

Gabby looked around her. She was on a second-floor walkway that went all the way around a courtyard below. She watched another man go into a different room, but a girl didn’t come out like she had. The courtyard was empty, and there were only two sets of stairs, one at the front and one at the rear. Gabby leaned her back against the wall next to the door, and slid to the ground. She curled her knees up in front of her, and waited. For what, she didn’t know.

Thirty minutes later, the man came back out of the room. He leered down at her with a half-smile. “What’s your name?”

Gabby ignored him, got up, and went back inside. Regina was dressed and sitting on the bed. She had flipped the TV on again. Gabby went to the phone and opened it.

Regina shook her head. “Don’t bother. It’s set up on two-way calling. You can’t dial anyone other than Rafael at the desk, and I wouldn't do that, if I were you."

Gabby dropped it like a snake about to strike. She lay on the bed, facing away from Regina. A few minutes later, the phone buzzed again. Regina answered it, turned off the TV, and got up.

"There's one coming up for you."

Gabby looked at Regina in horror as a knock came at the door and her roommate moved to answer it.

No, no, no…

Homicide Division
Flagler Street
12:30 p.m.

A folder was sitting on Eva's desk when she returned from lunch. It was the forensic report from the house where they'd found the van. She started reading while waiting for her partner to return.

Of greatest interest was the blood on the walls, but she quickly realized it wasn't going to help them much. The lab had run swabs from multiple locations in both bedrooms and come up with several different donors, which struck Eva as odd word choice, since the girls certainly didn't *donate* the blood.

Unfortunately, there was no match for either of their murder victims, and since they didn't have profiles for the two missing girls, they couldn't get a match for them. Eva looked up at Luis when he came in. "Forensics on the house is back."

"And?"

She shook her head. "It sucks!"

"Nothing?"

"There's a couple unidentified profiles, but neither of our murdered girls' blood is there."

He dropped into his chair. "You're right. It sucks. What about the van?"

"I guess they're still working on it."

"And the City Appraiser's office?"

"Nada."

"So we wait?"

She nodded. "We wait."

Room 203
Castle Hotel
1:00 p.m.

Gabby was lying on the bed, her eyes wet from tears, when Regina came back in the room. She heard the girl go in the bathroom, run some water, then come back out. The bed sagged as her roommate sat next to her. "Here."

Gabby opened her eyes to find a damp washcloth being held out to her. She took it, wiped her face, then her mouth, and finally her arms in a futile attempt to wash the smell off. Regina got up and went back to her own bed. "I'm not going to tell you it gets any easier, because it doesn't, but you find a way to cope. You have to or you'll lose yourself and your life."

The phone buzzed again, causing Gabby to involuntarily gag. Regina answered it, hung up, and looked at Gabby. "Take a walk."

Homicide Division
Flagler Street
3:30 p.m.

Luis picked up his phone. "I'm not waiting any longer. It's time to rattle some cages."

Eva smiled. "Which cage first?"

"The city."

Eva watched as he dialed, listened, then punched in an extension. He waited some more, then a voice. "Yes, my name is Detective Moreno and I was there this morning with my partner…" A pause. "You do? What is it?"

He grabbed a piece of paper and scribbled an address. "And that's the only one?" He nodded. "Okay, thanks."

Luis hung up and tore off the piece of paper. "Castle Properties owns a home in the western part of the city."

Eva stood. "Let me guess, she was just about to call you."

Luis laughed. "How did you know?"

"Like I said, just a guess."

Flagami Neighborhood
4:15 p.m.

Afternoon traffic slowed their progress, but they made it to the western part of the city in just over a half an hour. Flagami was a working class neighborhood with small single-story homes inside fenced yards.

The home registered to Estrada was directly across from Flagler Terrace Park, but more disturbing to Eva, it was only three miles from her daughter's school. When the detectives got out and crossed the street to the salmon-colored home, Eva noticed a distinct lack of activity in the neighborhood. "Not many people around."

Luis nodded. "I was just thinking the same thing. Maybe folks like to keep to themselves around here."

They walked up to the door and knocked. A minute later, the door opened and the detectives were surprised to be staring at Rafael Castro. "Yeah?"

Luis showed his badge. "Remember us, Mr. Castro?"

"Of course. You're the detectives harassing us at the hotel."

Luis managed a wry smile. "That's us. Can we come in and ask you a few questions?"

Castro hesitated, then stepped back. "Sure, why not."

Inside, the furniture bore a strong resemblance to the stuff they'd seen in the hotel lobby. Castro sat in a chair and sipped a beer. He waved his bottle at the couch. "Sit, if you want to."

Eva didn't want to. "Mind if I take a look around?"

"Help yourself."

While his partner checked the house interior, Luis opened his notepad. "This house belong to you?"

"Nope. I rent it from my boss."

"How long have you lived here?"

"Couple years, I guess."

"Anybody else live here with you?"

"Nope."

Eva came back in the living room and Rafael stared at her. "Find what you were looking for?"

"No."

"What was it you hoped to find, exactly?"

Eva smiled. "Just looking. That's all."

Luis closed his pad. "Thank you for your time."

Castro shrugged, but didn't get up.

"We'll let ourselves out."

Another shrug.

Outside, Eva climbed back in the car. "The place was clean, at least as far as the missing girls. There was no sign of them."

Luis started the car and pulled away. Eva took out her phone and called the Forensics lab.

"Forensics. Can I help you?"

"This is Detective Hernandez. Has the report on the Estrada van been finished yet?"

"No, ma'am. There still over at impound processing it."

"Okay, thanks." She hung up. "Looks like the van report won't be done until tomorrow. I think I'm going to go home and have dinner with my daughter."

Luis nodded. "Sounds good to me. I think I'm gonna remind my wife what I look like. Drop you at your car?"

"Perfect."

Saturday, March 7

Room 203
Castle Hotel
9:30 a.m.

Breakfast had been a fast food egg burrito and a bottle of water, but there was no shower that morning.

Rafael had dumped the food and scowled before leaving. “Neither of you made quota.”

Gabby had done her best to wash the smothering filth from the day before off in the sink, but no amount of soap would have succeeded. Her hair was greasy, and using an old rubber band Regina gave her, she had pulled it into a ponytail just to keep it out of her face.

The phone buzzed, and Regina hesitated, waiting to see if Gabby would answer it. Gabby had no intention of touching the thing. After several buzzes, Regina picked it up, listened, then pointed toward the door.

Relieved, Gabby stepped outside the room. A tall, thin man came up the stairs and passed her on his way into the room. Gabby leaned against the wall and closed her eyes.

She'd already spent a good deal of time studying the courtyard, looking for any vulnerability in the setup she could use for an escape. She was running the possibilities over in her mind when someone started yelling.

"Stop!"

Gabby's eyes flew open, and after scanning the courtyard, she spotted Sarah standing near the railing, a bedsheet tied around her neck. Rafael was running up the back steps toward her friend, screaming for her to stop. Everything shifted to a foggy slow motion, as Sarah looked toward Gabby, their eyes locking on each other.

Sarah appeared frozen in time, and Gabby heard her own voice yelling something at her friend, but the words were lost in the vision of Sarah climbing over the railing. Gabby pushed herself forward, waving her arms at her friend, who was still looking at her.

Then all at once, Sarah gave her a sad smile, and jumped. The sheet fluttered delicately, almost peacefully, behind Sarah as she dropped toward the courtyard. Then, suddenly and violently, it drew tight just before she reached the ground.

Gabby screamed, propelling everything into fast motion, as Sarah's body lay on the ground below. The torn sheet landed across her and covered her face, as Rafael reversed his climb and ran back down the stairs.

Girls came out of their rooms and two men appeared from somewhere else in the hotel. Gabby realized they weren't customers as they began yelling at the girls to get back in their rooms. Gabby was partway to the courtyard below when she was met by one of the men coming up the other direction. He pushed her backwards. "Go to your room!"

"That's my friend!"

He slapped her hard. "Now!"

Gabby allowed herself to be dragged back up and thrown inside her room. She lay in a heap by the door while Regina's customer stepped over her and ran. Overwhelmed by shock and guilt, she sobbed uncontrollably.

Surveillance Location
Castle Hotel
12:15 p.m.

Luis had agreed to take the first shift on their surveillance detail. He'd arrived just past ten that morning, parking down the street to the east and making sure he had a good view of the entrance to the hotel. With the help of binoculars, he made a note of the every person coming and going from the Castle Hotel, including license plate numbers when he could get them.

It wasn't Grand Central Station, but the flow of traffic was pretty consistent, and almost completely male. Luis wondered how this place hadn't produced more interest from the Vice Squad, but then he caught himself.

No tourists in this area, Luis!

He poured another cup of coffee from his thermos, checked his watch for the twentieth time, then went back to watching. He was there until four in the afternoon, so he slumped down in the seat and tried to relax, figuring he'd better get comfortable.

Room 203
Castle Hotel
1:30 p.m.

There been no noise from outside the room since the events of the morning, and this time when the phone buzzed, Gabby jumped for it. “Yeah?”

“You have a customer.”

“Where’s Sarah?”

There was no response.

“Is she okay?”

A moment’s hesitation. “You have a customer.”

The line went dead. Gabby threw the phone down and pointed at the door. “It’s me.”

Regina stood. “Did they say anything about your friend?”

Gabby shook her head.

Then came a knock.

****

An hour and a half later, the phone buzzed again, this time for Regina. Gabby left the room and walked over by the railing. On the courtyard below, Sarah's blood remained as a testament to Gabby's nightmare. She began to shake.

Oh, Sarah! I told you to stay alive.

Gabby stared at the blood for a long time, and eventually realized there wasn't *any* activity in the area below. She leaned out over the railing, looking for anyone watching, but found herself alone.

She moved down one side of the walkway toward the back stairs. When she reached the top of the rear staircase, she again leaned over, this time peering toward the front of the courtyard where the office was. Still no movement.

One step at a time, she made her way down the metal stairs, keeping her eyes glued to the office door. She was nearly to the bottom when a door slammed. She froze. Within seconds, the man who had been with Regina came down the front steps. Motionless, like a rabbit trying to avoid detection, she watched him reach the ground level and go out through the front door.

A minute or more went by, and another door opened. This time it was Regina coming out to talk, and she immediately spotted Gabby. Her eyes widened and she shook her head emphatically. Gabby could make out the words on her roommates lips.

No! Don't do it! Come back!

Gabby remained locked in place, now unsure whether to continue or retreat. She looked behind her at the hotel's rear exit, trying to determine if it was locked, but she couldn't tell for sure. Finally, she decided it was worth the risk. She owed it to Sarah to try, even if it got her killed.

Stepping off the bottom step, she saw Regina run back to the room, apparently not wanting to be caught watching. Gabby turned toward the back gate, and in three quick steps, was pulling on the door. It wouldn't give.

It's locked from the outside!

An arm wrapped across her throat and dragged her away from the doorway. "Where do you think you're going?"

From the corner of her eye, she recognized one of the men who had appeared when Sarah jumped.

There's guards! I should have known.

She struggled but he was much too strong. The arm across her throat was blocking her air passage and she grew faint. Then everything went black.

Surveillance Location
Castle Hotel
3:45 p.m.

Eva pulled up behind Luis at the surveillance spot. He got out of his car and came back to her as she rolled her window down. “Ready for me to relieve you?”

“Without a doubt.”

“You see anything interesting?”

He shook his head. “Afraid not. At least, no sign of the girls, but it’s clearly an illegal operation. Did the forensic report come in?”

“No, and it will be tomorrow at the soonest.”

“What? Why?”

“Apparently, the interior was clean enough that they got nothing. They started to disassemble the vehicle this morning and are hoping to find something in the undercarriage.”

“Dang. Well, it may take a couple days, but we should have no trouble getting a warrant for another look around the hotel for prostitution."

"Okay. Make sure you get your beauty sleep this afternoon and we'll see you at ten."

He laughed. "Will do. Good luck."

Room 203
Castle Hotel
5:30 p.m.

The phone had been quiet the rest of that afternoon, and Gabby had been able to lie on the bed to recover. Her arms and legs were scratched from fighting with the guard, who Regina informed her was named Jose, and her head pounded. Still, she was alive, something she wasn't sure would be the case when she was blacking out.

The door to the room burst open, causing both girls to jump. Javier came in, shut off the TV, and pointed toward the door. "Regina, get out!"

Regina scrambled to obey, ducking away from Estrada as she passed him, then closing the door behind her. Gabby could feel the pounding of her heart as Javier stared through her from the bottom of the bed, the pipe she'd heard about resting in his hand. "Didn't Regina tell you never to run?"

Gabby, trying to stay brave, nodded slightly.

"Didn't you believe her?"

"I… I was looking for Sarah."

"Outside the back gate?"

She didn't respond.

He moved along the side of the bed so quickly, she barely had a chance to react before he grabbed her hair, flipped her over on her face, and started hitting her with the pipe. Painful, lacerating strikes fell on her from all angles, and with her face buried in the pillow, it was pointless to scream.

The blows, the pain, and the blood, all came together into a nightmare she couldn't understand. Eventually, she stopped trying.

Surveillance Location
Castle Hotel
10:00 p.m.

Eva was glad to see Luis pull up. She got out and walked back to his car, sitting down in the passenger seat. “Get some rest?”

He nodded. “A little. Anything interesting going on here?”

“Pretty much the same as what you described, except for one thing. Estrada made an appearance this evening around dinner time.”

“Oh, yeah? Is he still there?”

“Nope. He left about forty-five minutes later.”

“Well, I imagine you’re hungry and tired, so I’ll take over. See you around four?”

Eva groaned. “Don’t remind me. Actually, I take that back. You *can* remind me by calling around three, okay?”

“Glad to do it. Later.”

She climbed out and headed for her car, which would take her home to bed. The one place she most wanted to be right then.

Sunday, March 8

Surveillance Location
Castle Hotel
9:45 a.m.

Eva had watched the sun rise behind her in the rearview mirror. Despite large amounts of coffee, she was ready for a nap. Unfortunately, there had been no sighting of either missing girl, and only the occasional car visitor to break the monotony.

Luis pulled up a few minutes early, so she got out and stretched, meeting him at the back of her car. "Nothing to report, I'm afraid."

"I was worried you were going to say that."

She smiled. "Sunrise was pretty, though."

"Well, that's something."

Eva's phone began ringing and she retrieved it from the front seat. "Hernandez."

"Yes Detective, this is Forensics."

Eva was quickly awake. “Is the van report done?”

“Yes, ma’am. I faxed it to your office a few minutes ago.”

“Give me the short version.”

“Okay. We found blood in two different locations. The first was the underside of the vehicle. There was a couple spots in the bed of the van that were rusted through and allowed blood to leak along the bottom. The second location was beneath the rubber seals around the back doors. We took them loose and swabbed them, finding blood in several places along the seals.”

Eva was nodding at her partner. “Now, the big question. Did you find a match?”

“Actually, we found two.”

Eva’s eyes widened as Luis became anxious. She held up her hand to keep him patient. “So, what were the matches?”

“The underside of the van bed matched Bonita Mendez. The door seals also matched the Mendez girl, but we also found a sample of Jessica Dawson’s blood.”

Eva pumped her fist. “Fantastic. Anything else?”

“We found two fingerprints on the bottom edge of the driver’s side mirror.”

“Any match?”

“A Rafael Castro.”

"Great. I'll get the rest from the report when I'm back at the office. Thanks."

She hung up. "The van has blood from both of our victims. We also have a fingerprint match to the manager."

Luis slapped the top of his car. "That's enough to bring charges, right?"

"Almost, I think. I'm going to the precinct. I'll get with the lieutenant after I've read the report."

"Good deal."

Eva jumped in her car and headed for the station. Suddenly, she was a lot less tired.

Office of Lieutenant Roberta Castillo 11:50 a.m.

"Close the door behind you."

Eva did, then sat down opposite the lieutenant, placing the forensic report on the desk between them. "Here's what we've got."

Castillo held up her hand, stopping Eva. "Let me make some notes." She pulled a notepad from her desk, grabbed a pen, then looked at her detective. "Okay, shoot."

Fifteen minutes later, Eva had laid out the case for charges against Javier Estrada and Rafael Castro. The lieutenant studied her notes for several minutes before speaking. "We've got one big problem."

"Which is?"

"Who was in the van with the bodies? Was Estrada driving or was it Castro? Were both there or neither? Maybe someone else dumped the bodies, which means they can claim that someone else did the murders."

Eva had anticipated those very things. "Estrada claimed the van was stolen, but that was disproved when it was found on one of his properties. His ownership at least makes him an accessory to the murders."

Castillo nodded. "I'll buy that, but what about the manager?"

"The fingerprints could put him in the vehicle. He's not as savvy as Estrada. What if we convince him we're going to pin both murders on him?"

"You mean to see if he rolls on Estrada?"

"Exactly."

The lieutenant pondered the idea for a minute, then nodded. "I'll get you a warrant to search the hotel again based on the blood in the van, and you can pick up Castro as a suspect based on the prints. Do an interrogation and lean on him to see if he'll give up his boss. But, I'm not getting a warrant for Estrada until we get something more concrete on him."

Frustrated, but knowing Castillo was right, Eva stood. "Okay. I'll call Luis and see if we can catch Castro at the hotel, and we'll need a couple units to serve the warrant with us."

"Done. Good luck."

Eva went directly to her desk and called her partner.

"Yeah?"

"We're getting a new warrant for the hotel, and we can pick up Castro. Have you seen him?"

"Yeah. He arrived about an hour ago."

"Good. If he leaves, follow him. We need him *before* we search the hotel so he can't communicate the news of a warrant to Estrada."

"You got it. When will you be here?"

"I'm hoping less than an hour."

"Keep me advised."

When she hung up, the lieutenant approached her desk. "Here it is." The warrant sheet landed on the desk in front of her. "Thanks, Lieutenant. I'm on my way."

Castle Hotel
Little Havana
1:00 p.m.

"Put your hands where I can see them." Eva had come into the hotel lobby with her gun drawn and the warrant in her pocket.

Rafael raised his hands, the surprise evident on his face. Luis moved behind the manager and pulled one of his hands, then the other behind him, snapping the cuffs on. Eva was talking the whole time.

"Rafael Castro, you are being detained on suspicion of first degree murder in the deaths of Bonita Mendez and Jessica Dawson. Furthermore, we have a warrant to search the Castle Hotel in connection with those deaths."

Castro was doing his best to remain calm. "You're crazy! I didn't kill nobody. You have to let me make a call."

"Not yet, I don't. Maybe later, huh?"

Luis handed his prisoner over to one of the accompanying officers. "Read him his rights, take him to the precinct, and hold him."

"Yes, sir."

When Castro was gone, the two detectives and three remaining officers began the search. Eva went out into the courtyard while Luis picked through the office. A couple girls were leaning on the railing. “Come down here, ladies.”

While they obeyed, Eva sent the officers around the rooms to collect the rest of the residents.

Twenty minutes later, six different women were sitting on the ground in the courtyard.

Eva had them gathered together in a group this time. “Okay ladies, this is how we’re going to handle our little problem. All of you are going downtown. When you get there, you’ll be given an opportunity to make a statement and answer some questions. If you cooperate…”

“Eva!”

She turned to see Luis waving at her. “Hold that thought, ladies.”

She walked over to where her partner was standing. “What’s up?”

“Come see what I found.”

He led her to the back office and to a shelf near the file cabinet. Carefully, he lifted a towel. Eva’s gaze went from the object to her partner. “Is that what I think it is?”

He nodded. They were looking at a piece of pipe, partially wrapped with duct tape and stained red. “Bag it, then call Castillo for a warrant on Estrada.”

“I’m on it.”

She returned to where the women sat. “Now, where was I? Oh, yes. If you cooperate, a statement is all I’ll need. However, if you feel compelled to test my patience, you’ll find yourself under arrest for prostitution. Comprendé?”

Each girl nodded.

Eva looked at the two officers and waved her hand at the group. “Let’s get them downtown.”

“Detective!”

Eva looked toward the far end of the hotel, up on the second floor, where the voice seemed to come from. “Where?”

The officer came to the railing. “Up here!”

The look on the officer’s face charged Eva’s adrenaline. “Coming!”

She ran to the back stairs, took them two at a time, and came to a stop at the entrance to the last room on the floor. “What have you…”

Words left her at the sight she encountered. Despite the blood and bruising, she recognized them immediately. “Are they…?”

He shrugged. “I was just going to check.”

Eva reached out and touched the nearest girl’s leg. “She’s warm!” The officer touched the other girl. “This one, too.”

Eva and the officer started to unwrap the bindings. Duct tape covered the eyes, ears, and mouths of both girls. Their hands were bound with rope, as were their feet. When the tape came off their eyes, Eva mouthed the words: *You’re safe now.*

Tears flowed down the side of their faces, as the two girls struggled to see each other. When the tape came off the first girl’s mouth, who Eva recognized as Gabriela, the girl whispered. “We stayed alive.”

****

Forty-five minutes later, Eva stood in the hotel parking lot with her partner as they watched the two girls loaded into ambulances. Inside her, a war was raging between the relief they’d found the girls alive and the anger of what they had endured.

An officer walked up to her. “Detective Hernandez?”

"Yeah?"

"We rechecked every room. There's no one else inside."

"Thank you. Forensics will be coming soon. Please secure the perimeter and protect it until then."

"Yes, ma'am."

Her phone rang. "Hernandez."

"Eva, I got your warrant."

"Thank you, Lieutenant. We'll activate a BOLO, then head over to his residence."

"Keep me informed."

"We will."

She hung up and looked at Luis. "Let's go get the S.O.B."

Home of
Javier Estrada
Little Havana
3:10 p.m.

The two detectives pulled up in front of the house on Palm Terrace, got out of their car, and drew their weapons. The possibility existed Estrada had gotten wind of events at the hotel and would be unwilling to give himself up.

Eva had no problem with taking him by force, in fact, right now she preferred it. They moved onto the front porch and took up positions on either side of the door. She nodded at Luis, who pulled the metal door open and banged on the wood entrance door.

Seconds later, it opened. “Yeah?”

They rushed in together, guns in Estrada’s face, pushing him to the floor. Luis rolled the startled man over and cuffed him. Once Luis had Estrada upright, he turned him to face his partner. Eva glared at him. “Javier Estrada, you’re under arrest for prostitution, assault, assault with a deadly weapon, torture, and anything else I can come up with.”

Estrada was clearly still in the dark about events at the hotel. “You guys are making a big mistake. You’ll regret this!”

Luis shoved the man outside and toward the car. Eva opened the car door and her partner pushed Estrada inside. Before she shut the door, she leaned in. “Estrada.”

He glared at her.

“I have a message for you.”

“Oh, yeah? From who?”

“Your niece, Gabriela.”

The color drained from the man’s face, and for the first time since she met him, Eva saw fear. She grinned at him. “She said to tell you *she’s still alive.*”

Eva slammed the door and Luis got into the driver's seat. "I'll take him downtown."

"Okay. I'll fill the lieutenant in and wait for the crime scene people. Pick me up later?"

"Will do."

Homicide Division
Flagler Street
5:30 p.m.

Later, at the division headquarters, Eva and Luis were in the observation room preparing to interview Rafael Castro. Eva wanted him to roll on Estrada, and thought she had a plan to make it happen. "So, you know what to do, right?"

"Yeah. Just give me a signal of some sort."

"When I stand up and go by the door."

"Works for me."

"Good. Here we go."

Eva went into the interrogation room, sat in the chair opposite Castro, and took out a tape recorder. "You don't mind if I record this, do you?"

"Ain't gonna be nothin' to record 'cause I got nothin' to say."

"Come now. There must be something we can agree to discuss. How about all those girls staying at the hotel who were having regular male visitors? Looks like prostitution to me, wouldn't you agree?"

"What my guests do on their time is none of my business."

"Well, what about the two ladies who we found tied and gagged in the hotel? You didn't know anything about them, either?"

"What two girls?"

"I see." She pulled a photo of the pipe out of her pocket and held it up for him to see. "Then I guess this would be a total mystery to you as well."

"Never seen it."

His reaction told her otherwise. "Well then, let's discuss Bonita Mendez and Jessica Dawson. Do you remember them?"

"Who?"

"The two women whose bodies were dumped on the beach. Their blood was found in Mr. Estrada's van. You know what else we found on the van?"

"You're going to tell me, right?"

"Your fingerprints."

Fear raced across his face, and Eva could tell she was getting somewhere.

He started to stammer slightly. "I ain't never driven that van."

"Really?"

Eva stood and went over by the door, leaning right next to the small window that looked out into the hallway. She stood there staring at Castro, waiting.

Castro ignored her at first, then looked up to see why their conversation had stopped. At that moment, Luis walked slowly by with Estrada in cuffs. The impact on Castro was immediate.

"Was that Javier?"

Eva pretended to be unaware, looking out the window. "Didn't I mention we picked him up?"

"No."

She could sense the wheels turning inside the man's head. She moved back over to her chair, turned it around and sat on it backwards, facing Rafael.

"Here's how I see this playing out. My partner is going to take Estrada into the next room for a statement and Estrada is going to play dumb, too. Then my partner's going to tell him the same things I just told you. But that's where things will change from your statement. Instead of ignorance, I think Mr. Estrada is going to claim surprise."

"He can't."

Eva raised an eyebrow. "Why not? I would."

Castro was showing signs of panic, so she pushed.

"If I was Javier Estrada, I'd say I was completely shocked by the evidence and I didn't know anything about a possible prostitution ring. I'd claim *you* were running it through the hotel without my knowledge. Then I'd claim that if any girls died, it was at *your* hands, as part of enforcing *your* prostitution enterprise. Finally, I'd claim the blood must have been in the van because *you* used it without my knowledge."

"He wouldn't do that."

Eva snorted. "Oh, I'm sure he would and probably is right now. On top of that, he can afford a high-dollar lawyer, but I'm guessing you'll be using one of our overworked public defenders, right?"

It only took a few seconds longer for Castro to figure it out. "I want a deal!"

"A deal? For what?"

"I'll give you everything you need to hang him. He's the one who hurt them girls and killed them other two!"

Eva reached over and picked up the tape recorder, looked at, then set it down closer to Rafael. "I've got lots of tape left, Rafael. Start talking."

"What about my deal?"

"That's up to the District Attorney and how good he thinks your information is, but I'll say this, I'd put my money on the DA and not your old boss."

Castro stared at her for a second, then started by declaring, "I didn't kill no one!"

She nodded and he began to talk.

Two and a half hours later, Eva had what she needed.

Monday, March 9

Jackson Memorial Hospital
Miami
8:30 a.m.

Eva knocked lightly at the doorframe to the semi-private room. A weak voice answered her. “Come in.”

Gabriela was in the bed nearest the door, and wanting to reassure her, Eva held up her badge. “Do you remember me?”

The girl’s head bobbed slightly. “I don’t remember your name, though.”

“It’s Eva. How are you making out?”

“Okay, I guess, considering.”

Eva pointed at the chair next to the bed. “May I?”

“Please.”

Eva put her badge away and sat down. “I wanted to come see how you’re doing and to make sure you know you’re safe.”

“I was told you arrested my uncle.”

Eva nodded. “And Rafael, too.”

“What about the guards? Jose and the other one?”

"My partner picked both of them up this morning."

They were quiet for a long time, but Eva could sense Gabriela had something on her mind. "What is it?"

"Would… would you mind holding my hand?"

Eva struggled against the tears threatening to overtake her and reached out, wrapping one of the young girl's hands between both of her own. "It would be my honor to hold your hand. You're a very brave girl, do you know that?"

A shrug. "I suppose. I just knew we had to stay alive until we got out of there."

"And you were right. How is your friend?"

"Ask her yourself. She's on the other side of that curtain."

Surprised, Eva reached back and pulled the partition drape open. Lying flat on the bed with a neck brace on, was Sarah. Her eyes rolled toward the detective and she managed a weak smile. "Hey."

Eva returned the smile. "Hey, yourself. How's the neck?"

"It'll be okay. I hyperextended it when I jumped off the second story."

"Jumped? I didn't hear about that."

There was motherly scorn in Gabriela's voice. "Darn fool tried to kill herself. Fortunately, she can't tie a decent knot!"

Sarah giggled slightly. "I think Gabby wanted to kill me herself when she saw me jump."

Eva reached out and took one of Sarah's hands. "Do you mind if I hold your hand, too."

Sarah's eyes were instantly overflowing. "I'd like that."

They sat together, Eva between the two girls' beds, one arm extending out to each.

It was impossible for the detective to miss the trauma in the eyes of both girls. Plain to see was the youthful innocence destroyed, the mental scars inflicted, and the emotional damage done. Eva's thoughts went to her Maria.

Could something like this happen to my daughter, despite my being a cop?

She knew the answer was yes, and the fact was, most of the events over the last couple weeks had taken place very close to her home. She'd had no idea how close the evil was, and it chilled her inside, producing an involuntary shudder.

Gabby's voice was weak but clear. "What happens next?"

"Well, first and foremost, you two have to get better."

"I meant to my uncle and Rafael."

Eva nodded. "I know you did. He'll be arraigned on Monday, probably ask for bail, but be denied because he's a flight risk to go back to Cuba."

"When will we tell our story to the court?"

Eva was stunned. "It's too soon for you to worry about stuff like that."

Gabby's voice was suddenly stronger. "He's not getting away with what he's done! I want to make sure he never has the chance to hurt anyone else."

Eva had encountered a lot of impressive people in her life, but the girl in front her was by the far the strongest individual she'd ever met. "You know what?"

Gabby shook her head.

"I plan to be there when you tell your story and reveal the truth of what he is."

Gabby smiled. "I'd like that."

"I'm here for both of you, okay?" She squeezed their hands. "And I'm going to prove it by smuggling some ice cream into this place!"

Gabby let out a small cheer.

Sarah giggled again. "I'd cheer too, but I can't move that much!"

Six Months Later

September 7

Miami—Dade County Courthouse 1:00 p.m.

The Miami-Dade Courthouse was one of the oldest buildings in downtown Miami. Six white pillars across the front supported a monument-like structure that narrowed to a multi-story column of offices rising toward the sky. It had been refurbished, but still carried the Old South charm of its prime. The inside was a different story, and the upgrades had equipped the old interior with everything a modern courthouse should have.

The court had come back from its Labor Day recess and the first case it had taken up was of defendant Javier Estrada. Eva and Luis had already testified, as had numerous experts. Earlier that morning, Sarah had testified. It had been difficult to watch, but she made it through. The afternoon session was to include Rafael Castro and Gabriela Estrada.

Like she promised, Eva was there for Gabby, just like she'd been there for Sarah. The three of them had become close since the day she'd helped unwrap them from their prison, and they had all looked forward to the time Estrada would answer for his actions. On top of that, Eva hoped the testimony would be a significant step in the healing process for both girls. Many of their scars still remained fresh.

The bailiff announced the judge, who came into the courtroom as everyone stood, then reseated themselves at the judge's direction. Dressed in a black robe, he looked toward the prosecution table and nodded. "Okay, Prosecutor. You can call your next witness."

"Prosecution calls Gabriela Estrada."

The doors at the back of the packed courtroom opened and Gabby came striding in. Her head was high and she was moving fast. Stepping through the swinging gate at the front, she crossed purposefully to the witness stand where she stopped in front of the bailiff.

He instructed her to raise her right hand. "Do you promise to tell the truth, the whole truth, and nothing but the truth, so help you God?"

Gabby looked directly at her uncle. "I do."

"Please be seated."

The prosecutor stood and approached Gabby. "Please state your name for the record."

"Gabriela Estrada."

"And your relationship to the defendant is what?"

"He is my uncle."

"Thank you. Now Miss Estrada, I would like you to take us through the events leading up to your rescue. Begin with how you found out about your uncle."

"Well, everything started when my mother passed away."

For the next hour and a half hour, Gabby told her story as Eva and the rest of the courtroom remained transfixed on her. In the silent chamber, her voice stayed strong and clear throughout her testimony, carrying the resolve Eva had come to know Gabby held inside.

Gabby's eyes remained dry, despite the fact that a few of the jurors and some of the observers were crying. She only choked up once.

"I looked over and Sarah was preparing to jump with a sheet around her neck. She hit the ground… It was awful and… I didn't know if she was alive or dead."

She produced a tissue, wiped away the tears, then continued until she was finished. When she finally stopped, a stunned silence hung in the room, not even the judge said anything. The prosecutor, who had returned to his seat, stood again with a dragging sound of the chair legs on the floor. "Miss Estrada. Is the man who perpetrated these crimes upon you in this courtroom today?"

"Yes, sir."

"Would you point at him please?"

Gabby nodded, stood, and leaned over the witness stand railing with her arm outstretched toward her uncle. "That's him there!"

Javier Estrada visibly cowered from his niece, and she kept the arm out, pointing at him for a long moment.

The prosecutor nodded. "Let the record show the witness pointed at the defendant. Thank you, Miss Estrada. No further questions, your honor."

As Gabby slowly retracted her arm, but remained standing and staring at her uncle, the judge asked if the defense had any questions for the witness.

"No, your Honor. Not at this time."

The judge turned to Gabby. "Young lady, you're excused, and thank you."

Gabby nodded and stepped down, walking defiantly toward the exit. When she got outside, Eva was waiting for her with Sarah, and the three embraced.

Eva raved to the two of them. "You both did great. You were so brave and I'm very proud of both of you."

Gabby was vibrating from the adrenaline surging through her. "What happens now?"

"Well, Rafael has to testify, and then closing arguments, and finally it goes to the jury."

"What is your best guess on when they will decide it?"

"It's incredibly hard to say. I would think the jury will get the case tomorrow, possibly the day after. Then, it's up to them."

Sarah was exhausted. "Let's get out of here!"

Eva put her arm around both girls. "Dinner is on me."

"And dessert?"

Eva laughed. "And dessert!"

Three days later

September 10

Miami-Dade
County Courthouse
11:45 a.m.

The jury got the case at nine-thirty that morning; they sent a note out at eleven-thirty. Gabby, Sarah, Luis, and Eva were all in the courtroom waiting when the judge had the jury file in. Once they were all seated, the judge spoke to the forewoman. "Madam Forewoman, I understand the jury has reached a verdict."

"Yes, your honor."

"Please hand the jury's verdict to the bailiff."

The bailiff crossed the silent chamber to the jury box and retrieved an envelope, then gave it to the judge. In a courtroom heavy with anticipation, the judge slid a single sheet of paper out, read it to himself, then looked at Javier Estrada. "The defendant will please stand."

Javier rose slowly, his attorney rising with him.

The judge wasted no time. "The defendant in the above entitled action, Javier Renaldo Estrada, is found guilty…"

The girls didn't hear the rest as they hugged and cried. Eva whispered in each girl's ear. "It's over."

Home of
Detective Eva Hernandez
Little Havana
5:15 p.m.

Eva had come home with her daughter's favorite takeout, and was sitting across the table from Maria on the back porch, watching her eat tacos. She had invited Gabby and Sarah to join them, but they'd opted to spend the evening together in the apartment they now shared.

Exhausted from the emotion of the day, Eva had just one thing left to do. The one thing driving her more than any other and she'd had on her mind for nearly eight months. It was a phone call, and it was time.

She dialed the number and listen to it ring several times, until finally a familiar voice picked up. "Hola?"

"Señor Mendez?"

"Si. Who is this?"

"This is Detective Eva Hernandez with the Miami PD."

"Yes, of course."

She smiled into the phone. "I promised you a phone call, do you remember?"

There was a moment's hesitation. "Is it done?"

"Yes, sir. He will never hurt anyone the way he hurt your daughter again."

A much longer silence followed, then a voice that cracked slightly. "It is a beautiful day, is it not, Detective?"

"As beautiful as your daughter, sir."

"Indeed. Goodbye, Detective."

"Goodbye, sir."

Eva hung up and wiped at her eyes.

"Why are you crying, Momma?"

She smiled. "Because it's a beautiful day."

Author's Note

As always, let me first thank each and every one of you who took time to read *MIAMI HOMICIDE*. Many of you have written since the publishing of *BOSTON*, and your encouragement has made the writing of the second *City Murders* much easier.

I'd like to thank Robert Toohey for his concise editing as well as my regular editor, Sam. You make me look better than I should!

The idea for this story was pulled from real events, and sadly, is much too common in our day and age. It's a terrible truth.

In the coming months, I plan on adding to the series with novels from Chicago, Dallas, Denver, and Seattle, among others. (Not necessarily in that order!)

God Bless, John
I John 1:9

Cover by Beverly Dalglish
Edited by Samantha Gordon, Invisible Ink Editing
Proofreading by Robert Toohey

Other Clean Suspense Books

By

John C. Dalglish

THE CITY MURDERS SERIES

BOSTON HOMICIDE - #1
MIAMI HOMICIDE - #2
CHICAGO HOMICIDE - #3

THE DETECTIVE JASON STRONG SERIES

"WHERE'S MY SON?" - #1
BLOODSTAIN - #2
FOR MY BROTHER - #3
TIED TO MURDER - #5
ONE OF THEIR OWN - #6
DEATH STILL - #7
LETHAL INJECTION - #8
CRUEL DECEPTION - #9
LET'S PLAY - #10

MIAMI HOMICIDE

HOSTAGE - #11
CIRCLE OF FEAR - #12
DEADLY OBSESSION - #13

THE CHASER CHRONICLES

CROSSOVER - #1
JOURNEY - #2
DESTINY - #3
INNER DEMONS - #4
DARK DAYS - #5
FAR FROM HOME - #6

TORN BY THE SUN - (HISTORICAL FICTION)

90118335R00171

Made in the USA
San Bernardino, CA
06 October 2018